A DEMON IN MY VIEW

PROSE SERIES 68

Guernica Editions Inc. acknowledges the support
of The Canada Council for the Arts.
Guernica Editions Inc. acknowledges the support
of the Ontario Arts Council.
Guernica Editions Inc. acknowledges the financial support
of the Government of Canada through the Book Publishing Industry
Development Program (BPIDP).
Guernica Editions Inc. acknowledges the Government of Ontario through
the Ontario Media Development Corporation's Ontario Book Initiative.

LEN GASPARINI

A DEMON IN MY VIEW

STORIES

GUERNICA

TORONTO · BUFFALO · CHICAGO · LANCASTER (U.K.)
2003

Stories in this book first appeared in *The Antigonish Review* and *lichen*.

Antonio D'Alfonso, editor
Guernica Editions Inc.
P.O. Box 117, Station P, Toronto (ON), Canada M5S 2S6
2250 Military Road, Tonawanda, N.Y. 14150-6000 U.S.A.

Distributors:
University of Toronto Press Distribution,
5201 Dufferin Street, Toronto, (ON), Canada M3H 5T8

Gazelle Book Services, Falcon House, Queen Square,
Lancaster LA1 1RN U.K.

Independent Publishers Group,
814 N. Franklin Street, Chicago, Il. 60610 U.S.A.

First edition.
Printed in Canada.
Legal Deposit – First Quarter
National Library of Canada
Library of Congress Catalog Card Number: 2003102903
National Library of Canada Cataloguing in Publication
Gasparini, Len, 1941
A demon in my view / Len Gasparini.
(Prose series ; 68)
ISBN 1 55071 179 2
I. Title. II. Series.
PS8563.A7D44 2003   C813'.54   C2003 900745 6
PR9199.3.G36D44 2003

CONTENTS

A Boy and His Cat. 7

Facts of Life 12

Cross of Flesh 31

Bet I Can Scare You 45

Wild Pitch 62

Off-Off-Broadway 78

A Lodging for the Night. 93

The Valentine 104

An Arabian Day's Entertainment. 106

Sign Language 108

Background Music 110

The White Sheep. 116

Amy Crissum. 132

The Succubus 152

For
Leslie Thompson, Sharon Roebuck, Dennis Priebe

A BOY AND HIS CAT

The boy opened his bedroom window till the sash was level with his eyes. "I want Kragol to jump out," he said.

His mother was shocked. "Don't be silly," she said. It was a twenty foot drop from the upstairs window to the driveway. Holding the cat in one arm, she put the back of her hand on the boy's forehead. He jerked his head back. "You've a little fever," she said. "If you don't go to bed right now, you can't play outside tomorrow. And I won't buy you that book of airplane pictures."

The conflict began when the boy refused to go to bed unless his mother read him a story. The boy's request was an innocent ruse. He knew his mother disliked reading bed-time stories. Twice she had tucked him in, then smoothed his blanket, making sure the sides of the blanket hung evenly over both sides of his bed. For some reason the boy liked the blanket to cover him that way. Every night he put his mother through this fussy ritual. (Friday nights she would let him stay up late to listen to the boy soprano sound of *"Calllll forrr Phil-lip Mor-eees!"* on the radio, with the clip-clop music of Ferde Grofé as background.) She thought he was coming down with the flu. His forehead did feel a bit feverish. Earlier, with the inducement of cherry Jell-O, she got him to swallow a teaspoonful of cod-liver oil. It was almost ten-thirty when she kissed him good-night a second time and left the bedroom door ajar to admit the light from the hallway. The boy was afraid to sleep alone in the dark. Sometimes he would sneak into his mother's bed.

The boy was four years old, an only child. He seldom saw his father. The father drove a taxicab six nights a week. He was also in the process of building a house for his family; so his days were busy too. The father took Sundays off. Since the boy's parents weren't churchgoers, Sunday mornings were given over to late breakfasts and the funnies. More often than not the father spent Sunday afternoons playing *bocce* or card games with his cronies. The mother compensated for this lack by overindulging her son. She was very fond of dressing him up.

Unable to sleep, the boy now decided he wanted his pet cat. He slipped out of bed and tiptoed in his pajamas to the top landing of the stairs. He sat down and called for his cat.

"Get in bed! Right now!" the mother said. Her voice carried a note of exasperation. She mounted the stairs.

"I want Kragol to sleep with me," said the boy. At night, the cat often curled up in the boy's bed.

The mother told him the cat was outside, catching mice. The boy could hear rain pattering on the windowpane. He wondered why the cat wasn't in the house.

"It's raining," the boy said. "Kragol wants to come in."

The cat had been a neighborhood stray. Several months ago it had followed the boy and his mother as they were walking home from the grocery store. The boy had stopped to stroke the cat, and it had meowed, its tail erect, begging for attention. It was a shorthaired ginger tomcat. All the way home the boy kept glancing over his shoulder to see if the cat was still following them. Each time he looked back he would say: *"Kragol-agol-agol."* He repeated those nonsense syllables over and over again, until they sounded incantatory. His mother was amused, and said he was talking cat-talk. The cat followed them home. The boy asked his mother if he could keep the cat. She said she'd ask his father.

Somehow the name Kragol had stuck. The cat was remarkable for the way it would play hide-and-seek indoors with the boy.

"I want Kragol," the boy insisted. "I want him to come here. Go an' get him."

The mother shot a disapproving look at him. "What do you say?"

"Please – " the boy murmured.

"Then will you go to sleep?"

He nodded.

"Promise?"

"Yes."

Realizing the hour was late, that she was tired, and that her son wouldn't be content till the cat was in bed with him, the mother felt compelled to fetch it. It was probably on the front porch, she thought, crying to be let in. While puttering about the kitchen and attending to her son, she had forgotten it.

The boy waited at the top of the stairs.

Presently she returned, cradling the cat in her arms. The cat's fur was slightly wet.

"Here's Kragol," she said, and dropped the cat gently on the bed. The boy smiled, and quickly scooped up the cat. He began to cuddle it. The cat twitched its tail and would not keep still. He tried to make it lie down under the blanket. Frightened, the cat meowed, resisting the boy's attention.

"Don't torment it," said the mother. "You'll get scratched."

Suddenly the cat squirmed out of the boy's hands and jumped off the bed. The mother reached down and picked it up.

"Maybe Kragol wants some milk," said the boy. His face showed disappointment.

"It's way past your bedtime. I want you to go to sleep," said the mother, with gruff finality.

"But I want Kragol to stay."

The mother put the cat on the bed, and held it there. She could feel how tense the cat was.

"I want the window open," said the boy.

The mother noticed that the rain had stopped. The room was warm and stuffy. "If I open the window," she said, "you must promise to be quiet and go to sleep. Do you hear me?"

The boy looked down, as if studying his blanket. The mother let him take the cat from her. She went over to the window, drew aside the curtain and raised the sash a few inches. There was no window screen. A scent of wet earth and flowering shrubbery wafted in. The eaves were dripping.

"Is that better?" she said.

"Can I put Kragol at the window? Please."

"What for?"

"So he can look out." He held the cat tightly. It meowed a few times.

The mother became annoyed. What next? she thought. Of course she realized her son's errant behavior was partly her fault. She gave in too easily to his whims and demands. She often wished her husband had more time to spend with their son. The boy seldom disobeyed his father. She found it difficult to discipline the boy when he misbehaved. All she could do was utter dire warnings: *Just wait till daddy comes home!*" or "*Wait'll I tell daddy what you did!*" Her threats usually worked, but she rarely carried them out. She recalled certain instances when the boy's waywardness warranted a spanking as well as a scolding – like the time he thrust his fist through a pane of glass in the back door at his Uncle Charlie's house because a cousin wouldn't let him play with a toy truck. His uncle drove him to the hospital to have his bleeding hand stitched up. And the time he got angry and flung a soup spoon at his grandmother, striking her just below the left eye. His father had spanked him soundly.

Seeing his mother's hesitation, the boy clambered out of bed with the cat, and dashed to the window. He tried to lift the cat onto the windowsill. The cat was very agitated, and one of its claws caught the boy's pajama sleeve. The mother snatched the cat from him.

"Get back in bed, or I'm going to put the cat downstairs," she said sharply.

The boy stood there, pouting.

"Well?" she frowned. "I'm waiting."

"No. I want Kragol to jump out. Let me hold him."

"Do you want Kragol to get hurt?" she said, stroking the cat. "Poor kitty."

"He won't get hurt. He can jump out. Please."

"If daddy was here, you know what he'd do – " she said, hoping to discourage him.

"He won't . . . he won't be mad . . . "

There was a pause. Standing there in his pajamas the boy looked defiant yet vulnerable.

A light breeze stirred the curtain.

"Please, mom," he pleaded. "Please."

His mother handed him the cat.

FACTS OF LIFE

The boys in my eighth-grade class at De La Salle were a sorry bunch. Most of them, including myself, had failed once. Some had even failed twice. A few sported peach fuzz or shaved at least once a week. There were no girls in my class. It was a Catholic school. Boys and girls were segregated. Certain boys (there were about 30 of us) stood out because of their size, pugnacity, or street savvy. "Big" Jim Bennett was built like a truck. At 15, he stood six feet tall and weighed 200 pounds. Big Jim was a natural athlete. He could knock the cover off a softball; score two hat tricks in a game of ice hockey; and gallop for a touchdown, dragging two opposing players with him. Big Jim dressed sloppily. He was one of those kids whose lips move when they're reading. John Holland was another: 15, freckle-faced, with a shock of red hair. Holland's quickness of temper was matched by his uncanny ability to do arithmetic in his head faster than any of us could do on paper. Whenever he grinned, you could see as much of his gums as his yellow teeth. And there was Don Belleperche; also 15. Shrewd, lazy, and vain about his clothes; habitually combing his black wavy hair. Belleperche wore his pegged trousers low at the waist, and buckled his suede belt at the hip. He was handsome in a hoodlumish way, and knew things boys his age weren't supposed to know. At recess, he smoked in the alley beside the school; rarely joined in our schoolyard games, and acted as though we didn't exist. However, he had one peculiarity which made him vulnerable. He always had a hard-on in class. Whenever the teacher asked him a question, all heads would turn toward Belleperche who pretended not to hear his name called. The teacher would repeat it sharply. Belleperche would emit a nervous little cough, and then slowly rise to his feet clutching a textbook to conceal the erection straining his fly.

Our teacher was Brother Alban. He was also the principal. He was in his late thirties, dark-complexioned, of medium height, in good physical shape, and balding. Like the other Christian Brothers at De La Salle, he wore a black cassock over his shirt and trousers. His breath and nicotined fingers attested to the fact he was a heavy smoker.

Brother Alban inspired fear and respect. There was talk he'd once been an amateur welterweight boxer. He looked it, too. He had a boxer's hard, squarish hands. We were afraid to anger him. One morning some knucklehead who seldom did his homework told Brother Alban to "go to hell." Brother Alban decked the kid with one swift smack on the face. Although Brother Alban wasn't a stickler for rigid discipline, he didn't take any guff from us. Nor did he show favoritism. He was tough but fair.

The boys in my class were at that pimply age when the so-called facts of life were of special interest. Not all of us had sex on the brain, though. Big Jim, Elso Martinello, Billy Predhomme, myself, and a few others were more concerned with sports and National Hockey League stats. We argued whether Gordie Howe was better than Maurice "The Rocket" Richard. We kept track in the newspaper of the number of saves Terry Sawchuck, Gump Worsley, Jacques Plante, Harry Lumley, Sugar Jim Henry, and Al Rollins made during the season. We bet money on which team – Detroit or Montreal – would win the 1955-56 Stanley Cup.

Of course we were curious about girls; but none of us had girl friends. We certainly didn't play with girls in the schoolyard. Our only interaction with them was mutual name-calling, especially when they got in the way of our softball and touch football games. The nuns and Christian Brothers at De La Salle kept a watchful eye on us.

There was one boy who had a remarkable talent for mimicking a girl's voice. His name was George Goulet. We called him "The Ghoul." He was a tall, skinny, anemic-looking 14-year-old, and a bit of an oddball. The Ghoul took guitar lessons, and enjoyed telling dirty jokes and instigating trouble. His idea of fun was to call some boy on the phone and talk obscenely to him in a convincingly girlish voice. I disliked The Ghoul, but listening to him talk on the phone was a riot. Sometimes, if we had nothing better to do, Elso and I would go to The Ghoul's house on a weekend night, when his parents were out. His fridge was always stocked with beer and soda pop, the cupboards crammed with potato chips, Fig Newtons, Ritz crackers, pretzels.

With his sexually suggestive spiel, The Ghoul would excite some boy on the phone, and then induce him to visit the house of a girl whose address The Ghoul knew. Nine times out of ten his deception worked. We would dash over to the street the girl lived on (two or three blocks away), hide behind a parked car or a tall hedge, and wait for the boy to knock on the girl's front door.

The girl whose address The Ghoul often used was that of Doris Potts. Doris was 15. She was big, ungainly, bucktoothed, and had the biggest pair of boobs. She was so boy-crazy, that her mother had to meet her most days after school. Doris had a habit of following boys home. She would loiter in front of a boy's house, pretending she had lost something. Eventually she'd get tired and walk away.

One Friday night The Ghoul phoned Don Belleperche, and tried to trick him. In less than a minute The Ghoul's face reddened, and he angrily slammed down the receiver. Elso and I kept asking him what Belleperche had said, but he refused to tell. On Monday, at school, word got around that Belleperche had the crabs.

The Ghoul had a morbid fascination with penis sizes. He wasn't a queer, but he seemed to think the size of one's penis indicated one's character – the same as I judged a guy by the way he threw a ball. If he threw like a girl, I thought less of him.

It was a truth generally acknowledged by teenage boys that some penises were envied, some ridiculed, and some bragged about. Whenever The Ghoul was with a group of boys, he brought up the subject of penises in a crudely joking way. The Ghoul knew how to provoke a situation. He exerted a certain influence because, despite his puny build, he was well hung. He could easily rouse suspicion about any kid who was timid or innocent about sex. "I bet mine's bigger than yours," he would challenge the boy. If the boy laughed nervously and said nothing to disprove The Ghoul's claim, other boys would join in the fun. Amidst the horseplay and idle threats, the empty boasts and stupid arguments, they would often gang up on the boy, and pull down his trousers and underpants. Big Jim sometimes joined in. When he pinned you to the ground, it was impossible to break loose. If a boy's penis was un-impressive in size, and he got angry at having it forcibly exposed, then he lost face and became a target for ridi-cule. It was a kind of initiation. Getting along with the boys required character and a sense of humor.

Pat Amlin was one boy who resisted the group's initia-tion. Pat was unassuming yet stubborn. Most of the boys in our class considered him a brownnose and a sissy. One day after school Big Jim, Elso, Billy, Ed Bechard, Earl

Beneteau, Louis Marcuzzi, myself, and three other boys
were playing touch football in a vacant lot. The Ghoul
was there, too. He had a tin whistle, and was acting as
linesman. Sitting alone at the edge of the lot was Pat Amlin,
looking bored and uncomfortable. Pat owned a pocket-
knife I wanted the worse way. The knife was butterscotch-
colored and shaped like a bowling pin. I had offered him
money for it; tried to swap my collection of hockey cards,
a compass, a cigarette lighter – but to no avail. Finally he
was keen on seeing a pair of handcuffs I had. I didn't tell
him the handcuffs were rusty and keyless.

After our game, in which touch had turned to rough-
house, everyone was sweaty, bruised, and making wise-
cracks. I could see Pat was eager to leave. I was too.
Playing sports with the boys was one thing, but horsing
around with them afterwards often resulted in a fist-fight.

"Where you guys goin'?" Big Jim said gruffly.

"Hey, Pat – catch." Elso flung the football at him.

Pat made a clumsy grab for the ball but it bounced off
his chest.

"Sign him up," Bechard gibed.

"Yeah, for pocket pool," said Marcuzzi. The others
laughed.

"Leave him alone," I said, and started walking away,
expecting Pat to follow.

"Who asked for your two cents?" Elso called after
me. I stopped.

"No one asked him," Pat cut in. "Just because you can
catch a stupid football doesn't mean you're a hero."

"Chew on this, you fuckin' fairy," said Elso, clutching
the crotch of his grass-stained trousers.

"C'mon, Pat, let's go," I urged him.

"When I eat, I wanna meal, not a snack," Pat retorted.

There was a chorus of jeering *oohs* and *aahs*. Pat was
in deep trouble now. Elso became so enraged, he lunged

at Pat threateningly. Pat backed away several feet. The others looked on, guffawing and shouting, eager to see an unfair fight.

"Lippy asshole, ain't you? Goddamn little bed wetter." Elso rushed at Pat and gave him a vicious shove, knocking him down. As Elso was about to pounce on him, Big Jim held him back, and began counting the seconds, like a boxing referee.

"ONE . . . TWO . . . THREE . . ."

"I wonder if his dick's as big as his mouth," The Ghoul said.

"Let's find out," Bechard suggested.

"Buzz off!" said Pat, who was hunched on the ground. He seemed determined to remain there. Big Jim kept counting.

"Get up, shithead," Elso sneered. The others clustered around Pat, taunting him.

"Leave him alone," I said.

" . . . NINE . . . TEN. NIGGER PILE!" Big Jim shouted, signaling a free-for-all.

Pat was buried, kicking and screaming, under an avalanche of bodies. The boys hurled themselves upon him and upon one another – yelling, scrambling, laughing. Some took running dives into the pile, landing with a thud on those who were trying to get up. The Ghoul was beaming with excitement. I saw him sneaking a hard kick at Pat's leg. I stood there, watching, wondering if Pat's knife would fall out of his pocket.

"Take his pants off!" The Ghoul shouted.

Three boys held Pat down. Bechard and Marcuzzi tugged at Pat's trousers. Pat was cursing, thrashing furiously. I saw his hairless white legs.

"It looks like a peanut!" said Bechard.

"Half a peanut," The Ghoul added.

They released Pat. Bored, some of the boys walked away.
Pat was having a red-faced shit-fit. Suddenly he pulled out
his knife and jabbed Elso in the shin. Elso gave a yelp.

"You sonofabitch!" Elso took a swing at him and missed.
"Drop that fuckin' knife!"

Pat held onto the knife till Big Jim grabbed him in a
hammer-lock and wrenched it out of his hand. Elso picked
up the knife and flung it over a fence, into someone's backyard.

"WHAT'D YOU DO THAT FOR?" I exclaimed.

Pat ran off, cursing. Elso examined the red pinprick on
his shin. Beneteau called me a "spoilsport." Billy shook
his head in disgust, and said I was "Mister Death." Soon
everyone drifted off. I went looking for the knife but
couldn't find it.

All of us were virgins except Don Belleperche. Despite
The Ghoul's dislike of Belleperche, we thought Belleperche
was a cool character, even though he didn't chum around
with us.

There was one girl who had a bad reputation at De La
Salle. Her name was Helen Soulliere, a 14-year-old with
baby fat and short brunette hair. Helen wasn't what you'd
call pretty, but she had a slovenly charm. She always had a
sleepy smile on her face, and her clothes looked as though
she slept in them. Helen's parents must have been poor,
because Helen wore clothes that looked like flimsy hand-
me-downs a size too small, which made her nubile breasts
and round buttocks conspicuous. There was always a
hickey on her neck. Helen's notoriety concerned an incident that happened after school. A nun caught Helen necking with some highschool freshman in a toilet stall in the
girls' lavatory. Helen was suspended from school for two
weeks. She and Belleperche were cousins.

Helen was common. There were two older girls who were legends in the neighborhood. Both of them had acquired an almost mythical status for their promiscuity. Their names were Frenchie and Dirty Gertie. They were both in their late teens, and their very names evoked the sexual fantasies of adolescent boys. Their specialty was the gang bang. It was said that Frenchie took on ten guys at a stag party. And it was said that Belleperche had "sloppy seconds" with her. I saw Frenchie and Dirty Gertie on the street now and then. Frenchie was the shorter of the two. Both of them were busty. They wore tightfitting clothes and a lot of makeup. They certainly looked sexy; but they weren't beauty queens.

The Ghoul had a crush on Helen Soulliere. He even scratched her initials on his desk.

"I wouldn't touch her with a barge pole," Marcuzzi said. Marcuzzi had kinky hair and thick lips. He often farted in class; in fact, he could fart at will.

The Ghoul called Marcuzzi "Pig-Lips" behind his back. It was Marcuzzi who said The Ghoul phoned Helen every night and disguised his voice so she wouldn't hang up on him.

One Saturday afternoon I ran into The Ghoul on the corner of Wyandotte Street and Louis Avenue. We stood chatting beside a bus stop. The Ghoul bragged he was screwing Helen Soulliere. Of course I didn't believe him. A bus soon came along and stopped. The Ghoul looked as if he was going to board it. When the door of the bus opened, The Ghoul put one foot on the step-well, laced up his shoe, then thanked the bus driver and backed away. I thought it was a clever stunt. We both laughed. Suddenly I saw Don Belleperche across the street. He was with two older guys. Belleperche saw us.

"Hey, dipshit!" Belleperche sneered. The Ghoul froze. A trapped animal. They crossed the street, heading toward us. One of the older boys spat on the sidewalk. The Ghoul's chapped lips began to twitch.

"I hear you been bad-mouthin' my cousin," said Belleperche.

"Not me! No – I haven't – " The Ghoul stammered.

"Sayin' she's a slut, an' gives blowjobs."

"I never said that!" The Ghoul looked at me for support.

"I heard different," Belleperche said, jabbing The Ghoul hard in the chest.

The Ghoul stepped backward. "It's a lie!"

"You know what, George? You even look like a fuckin' ghoul. A ghoul with a big ghoul mouth. Maybe I should knock all the goulash outta you."

The two older boys laughed harshly. The Ghoul just stood there, stuttering his denials and biting his lower lip.

The taller of the two older boys took a step toward me.

"Leave him alone. He's cool," said Belleperche.

Both older boys, about 17, looked mean and tough. Hard rocks. The tall one had a duck's-ass haircut and was wearing motorcycle boots and a black leather jacket with silver studs in the collar. The other had a cigarette tucked behind his right ear. He was chewing on a toothpick and constantly spitting.

If Big Jim was here, I thought, he'd kick their asses out their mouths. I made no effort to defend The Ghoul.

It was over in less than a minute. Belleperche punched The Ghoul twice in the face and once in the stomach. The Ghoul tottered backward, then sank to his knees, gasping for breath. The kid with the toothpick flicked his cigarette butt at him.

"Nice seein' you, George. You fuckin' creep," Belleperche scoffed.

All three walked away, laughing.

His body trembling, The Ghoul looked almost comical as he tried to straighten himself up. He spluttered out some words I couldn't understand. His mouth was full of blood.

I was doing my homework when I heard a song called "Heartbreak Hotel" on the radio. It was sung by someone named Elvis Presley. The quavering, sensual voice of Elvis, and the music and lyrics so fired my being, that I went outside, jumped onto my Schwinn bicycle (with whitewall balloon tires), and rode around aimlessly for an hour, humming the tune over and over. Rock 'n' roll had just rocked my soul, and I knew that my soul wanted more rock 'n' roll.

Brother Alban called us animals, dunces, slackers, zombies, louts, nail-biters, ass-scratchers and, in kinder moments, Windsor's future auto workers. We weren't sure whether he was being sarcastic or not. Big Jim said he was quitting school to get a job after he finished grade 8. So were Marcuzzi, Elso, and John Holland when they turned 16.

With a class like ours, Brother Alban had to be tough. He certainly let us know who was boss. Sometimes he had to remind us with a leather strap. Or flinging brushes and pieces of chalk. Or using a wooden paddle. The latter punishment was humiliating as well as painful. Charles Dickens would have been appalled. Brother Alban would call you to the front of the classroom, order you to empty all objects (combs, wallets, handkerchiefs) from your back pockets, and then order you to bend over (ass to the class), with your head against the wall, a few inches under the chalk ledge, and your hands on your knees. He would swing the paddle with all his might, and give you a re-sounding whack on your behind. His momentum and follow-through plus the paddle's impact lifted his heels and yours off the floor at the same time, causing your head to reflexively jerk upward and hit the chalk ledge. You often lost your balance and wobbled a little. Brother Alban never administered more than two whacks. Marcuzzi said he once got whacked so hard, he had splinters in his ass.

We respected Brother Alban because we feared him. He was a good teacher, he took a genuine interest in our progress, dismal though it was. Unlike Brother Edmund who taught manual training. What an enigma he was! Flabby, finicky, fainthearted (he couldn't stand the sight of blood, and panicked if anyone cut himself), ingratiatingly pleasant – too friendly, in fact, which made us suspicious of his motives. In the manual training room, with its smell of sawdust and varnish, Brother Edmund would flit about with his yardstick, nodding, smiling, advising, or hovering over some boy (usually Pat Amlin who was all thumbs, like me), and flattering him on his woodworking project. He was always patting our backs, touching us. Billy swore that he saw Brother Edmund giving Pat an affectionate pat on the ass. "It looked like he was copping a feel," Billy said later. Of course we heckled Pat. Earl Beneteau took to goosing him. When Elso brandished a coping saw and threatened to cut off Pat's dick, The Ghoul chortled: "If you can find it. *Ha-ha!*" We also learned that Brother Edmund was fond of going on bicycle rides with certain boys after school. Pat was one of those boys. Toward the end of the Lenten season Brother Edmund was transferred to another grade school.

On the morning after Ash Wednesday, Brother Alban announced that Father Poisson was coming to our class to give an important talk.

"On what?" asked Bechard.

Brother Alban frowned. "Practising self-control."

We regarded the news of Father Poisson's visit as a chance to goof off. As though anticipating that probability, Brother Alban warned us to be on our best behavior. Yet we knew that he would use the priest's visit as an opportunity to relax in the staff lunchroom.

Although we believed in God, some of us already harbored doubts about the existence of heaven, hell, purgatory, and limbo. I could count on the fingers of both hands those of us who regularly attended church on Sundays.

We were all more or less familiar with Father Poisson, or Father "Fish," as we called him. He was a short, pudgy yet dapper man with a cherubic face, who spoke with a lisp in a cartoon voice that sounded as if he were inhaling helium instead of air. He was also the choirmaster at Immaculate Conception Church. According to The Ghoul, Father Poisson had been trying for months to persuade him to join the church choir. (The Ghoul said that Father Poisson drank gallons of the Eucharist wine.) Father Poisson was also in charge of the C.Y.O. (Catholic Youth Organization), and he was active in the Sodality and the church bingo. It was common knowledge that he was very popular with the church-going widows of his parish.

In walked Father Poisson – black suit and clerical collar – smiling warmly and radiating goodwill. He and Brother Alban exchanged greetings. Our class stood up noisily and wished him good morning. Brother Alban left the room for a moment, and returned with a glass of water, which he placed on his desk. Brother Alban then sat down, with a stern expression on his face.

Father Poisson made the sign of the cross, and began to speak in a lofty yet friendly tone, clasping and unclasping his small white hands. Because of his lisp it was difficult to understand everything he said. Afraid they would snigger, some of the boys clenched their jaws

or covered their mouths with their hands. Brother Alban
shifted nervously in his chair.

"As you all know, ye*th*terday was Ash Wednesday – the
first day of Lent," said Father Poisson. "Ashes to ashes,
du*th*t to du*th*t. Du*th*t thou art, and to du*th*t thou shalt
return. Lent is a time for prayer, penitence, and fasting. I
hope all you boys were pure enough in heart to receive
the Ble*th*ed Sacrament at Mass." He paused, as if waiting
for our affirmative response. There was silence, then a
meager show of hands. (I knew Bechard was lying. He
shoplifted 45 rpm records at Kresge's.) Father Poisson's
face clouded with disappointment. "Ye*th*, well, the meaning of Lent," he said, "is the purification of heart and mind.
We purge ourselves of sin and *th*elfishne*th* with *th*elf-de-
nial and prayer. Holy Communion creates in u*th* the desire to do God's will and brings u*th* into intimate and loving
contact with the source of all holiness; and more than
anything el*th* spiritualizes our character and fills it with a
wonderful strength. Bodily fasting and *th*elf-di*th*ipline gives
u*th* control over ourselves. And the Holy Sacrament brings
about that purity of heart, and that is the goal of Lent."
Licking his lips, Father Poisson reached for the glass of
water. He took a sip, then gulped down the rest.

Marcuzzi emitted a half-stifled laugh. Brother Alban
warned him with a frown.

"It's a bit warm and stuffy in here," Father Poisson
sniffed. "Will someone please open a window."

Brother Alban opened one of the windows several
inches.

"Ah, that's much better. Thank you, Brother Alban,"
said Father Poisson. He handed Brother Alban the empty
glass. Brother Alban left the room.

"I've come here this morning to talk about you." Father Poisson smiled at the class. "Now, what do we mean
by *teenagers?*" (There was sniggering.) Father Poisson

paused, then continued: "The teens begin at thirteen and end at nineteen. The teens are, in fact, the time of life when age in actual years is of the greatest importance. Boys often start going with girls because they think it's a grown-up thing to do. They think they'll be envied and admired by their friends if they seem to be popular with the girls; but often they would really prefer to be with other boys. During the years of your adolescence there's a danger that sexuality will be con*th*idered more a burden than a gift. Between the ages of thirteen and fifteen, as all of you boys are, a proper understanding of sex, or the *facts of life*, is ne*theth*ary. (Brother Alban came back with a much larger glass of water. He placed it on his desk, then slipped quietly out of the room.)

"Pleasure is something that lives in the body," said Father Poisson, "and it's there without our desiring it. For example, perfume smells ni*th* whether we wish it or not. In this case, we can usually get away from the source of pleasure if we so will it. But this is not always the case with venereal, or sexual, pleasure. Remember: sexual pleasure often comes against your will. To bring about deliberately even the slightest sexual pleasure, alone or with someone el*th*, or to take a delight in it with your will if it is accidentally aroused, is always a mortal sin . . ."

"Wow!" exclaimed Belleperche, with mock astonishment.

"Ye*th*, it's a mortal sin," repeated Father Poisson. "To take a willful delight in sexual pleasure, whether the pleasure is complete or incomplete, is a mortal sin."

"What about dreams, Father?" said Bechard.

"Not now, my son," said Father Poisson. "I'll answer all your questions later." He took a sip of water. "Now here's a question for you. Let's say that John, who is fourteen – "

"Who – me?" said John Holland. There was laughter.

"No, not you," said Father Poisson, "I'm just using an example. Let's say that John decides to take a peek into the girls' dre*th*ing room at the gym. John knows he shouldn't do so, but he expects to get a sexual thrill. Yet he sees nothing to excite him because the girls have individual dre*th*ing compartments. Now I ask you – does John sin?"

"No – he doesn't," John Holland blurted out.

Pat Amlin waved his hand. Father Poisson nodded to him.

"Yes, he does sin," said Pat, "because he's thinkin' about a thrill."

"Right, my son," said Father Poisson. "John is committing a mortal sin, which is the *willing enjoyment* of unlawful sexual pleasure, in action, desire or thought. What's the matter?" Father Poisson looked at Belleperche, who was making guttural sounds with his hand over his mouth.

"I gotta toothache, Father," Belleperche muttered.

"I'm *th*orry to hear that. If you think of the sufferings of Jesus between the Last Supper and his death on the Cross, your toothache will seem infinitesimal in comparison." Father Poisson took a long drink of water, then glanced at his watch. "As I was saying, anyone who knowingly and willingly engages in immodesty, unchastity and lewdness commits a serious sin because he becomes delinquent with respect to God. Sexual acts are beautiful and holy in marriage, but outside marriage they're shameful and vicious. You must always remember that.

"Self-satisfaction, self-abuse, or masturbation – the solitary sin – is the most widespread delinquency among teenage boys. No act should be done with the deliberate intention of causing a sinful pleasure in the genitals. Masturbation is a terrible sin and leads to the development of dreadful passions. You must never touch your*th*elf indecently, and never, never, never allow another per*th*on to touch you indecently. Remember that the eye of God is all-seeing. No matter where you are, whether in the most hidden part of the garden, or in an alley, or the bath-room, or on the street, God is there, watching you, and you mustn't do any action which you should wish to hide from the eye of God. Many teenage boys become in-volved with masturbation through seduction, per*th*onal hygiene, or sports . . ."

"Sports?" Big Jim said, with shocked disbelief.

"Ye*th*. Many boys fall into the habit of stimulating their genital organs, even though they know it's a sin. Anyone guilty of this sin must turn away from it. The sacrament of penance not only wipes out the filthy stain of your sin, but also gives you a healing strength to resist temptation and to avoid committing other sins of impurity. Mastur-bation is a grave moral disorder. Don't forget that. And don't feel embarrassed to confe*th* your sins to a priest. He only wants to help you. Saint Paul said: 'The body is not for fornication, but for the Lord. Your body is the temple of the Holy Ghost.' And it's a terrible sin to pro-fane it. Remember: lust is one of the seven deadly sins. It's the source of other sins, and it's fatal to your spiritual progress . . ."

The Ghoul suddenly waved his hand.

"Ye*th*, George. What is it?"

"What are the other ones?" asked The Ghoul, half-smirking.

"The other ones?" Father Poisson looked puzzled for a moment. "Oh, you mean the seven deadly sins. Don't you know? (The Ghoul shook his head.) Who can tell George what they are? I'll give you a hint. *Pride* is one of them. Who can name the other five?"

"Stealing?" said Bechard.

"*Thou shalt not steal* is a commandment," said Father Poisson.

"I know, I know!" Pat said, waving his hand excitedly. "Envy, anger . . ."

"Ye*th*, go on," said Father Poisson. Pat cupped his chin in his hand and shook his head slowly. "Very good. But I'm afraid we're straying from the main subject." Father Poisson glanced at his watch.

"What are the other three?" asked John Holland.

Father Poisson looked at him with annoyance. "Sloth, gluttony, and covetousness," he said dryly. After a pause, he said: "I've been talking to you about the dangers of sexual pleasure; but I think we should go over those parts of the body called the genital organs – the ones that often get u*th* into trouble . . ." (Some of the boys sniggered. Belleperche asked permission to go to the lavatory.) "The male organs of reproduction are mostly external. The testicles and the peni*th*. The testicles are two small glands su*th*pended in a sack, or scrotum. They prod*ooth* sperm that's ejaculated through the erect peni*th*. This happens in the marital act or during *th*leep. As you probably know, the peni*th* is the main source of sexual pleasure in the male. Any stiffening of this organ should be checked by prayer, by exercise, by a change of body position, or even by thinking about your schoolwork. Remember: temptation is always in the senses; virtue and victory are in the will.

"Someone asked about dreams. I pre*th*ume that per*th*on was referring to nocturnal pollution. Well, the loss of semen during the night when you're a*th*leep is sometimes involuntary; but sexual dreams frequently accompany it. Try not to lie on your stomach in bed or fall a*th*leep in that position, because the friction of your genitals against the mattre*th* might cause you to have an erection, which will either wake you up or lead to nocturnal pollution. Anyway, those dreams shouldn't worry you if they're beyond the control of your mind and will. If you wake up during the emission and stop any action that may be causing it, then you haven't sinned. (Belleperche returned, smirking. As he passed my desk, I could smell tobacco smoke.) The devil always finds ways to tempt you. The best thing to do is go back to *th*leep." He took another drink of water, emptying the glass. "Will one of you boys please fill this glass with cold water. The air in this room is making me thirsty."

In four quick strides Pat Amlin was standing before Father Poisson, who handed him the glass. With a glow of satisfaction, Pat hurried out of the room.

"I think we have time for a question or two," said Father Poisson, smiling.

"I gotta question, Father," Marcuzzi said, waving his hand.

"Ye*th*?"

"What's *e-mission* mean?"

A few boys tried to answer at the same time.

"Pardon." Father Poisson frowned slightly.

"E-MISSION. I dunno what it means."

Ye*th*, well, an emission is the di*th*charge of semen from the erect peni*th*."

Pat returned, holding the glass of water with exaggerated care. Father Poisson took a deep drink. As Pat walked back to his desk, Elso tripped him, and he stumbled. Father Poisson looked questioningly at Elso.

"I was just stretchin' my leg, Father," Elso said, feigning a look of innocence. "My leg fell asleep."

Just then the door opened wide enough for Brother Alban to poke his head in.

"Come in, Brother Alban, come in," said Father Poisson. He looked at his watch. "Well, boys, I'm afraid we've run out of time."

Brother Alban stood beside the priest. "I hope they behaved themselves, Father. They can be annoying at times."

"No, no, no – not at all. A good class. Very attentive.

Ye*th*, good Catholic boys. If my talk with them was instructional and edifying, then I've served our Savior."

"Thank you, Father," Brother Alban said, motioning to us.

"Thank you, Father," our class repeated in unison.

Father Poisson smiled. "Remember," he said, "the clean of heart are those who are in the state of grace and in the friendship of God. It was Saint Augustine who said – 'There is no salvation out*th*ide the Roman Catholic church.' Ye*th*, well, I hope to see all you boys in church every Sunday." He made the sign of the cross. "In the name of the Father, and of the Son, and of the Holy Ghost. Amen."

The school bell rang. It was lunchtime.

CROSS OF FLESH

Although certain experiences and images linger in the memory, the emotions with which we realized them are easily forgotten. Yet what we see is often a question of what we feel. When I was 15, I went on my first date. Looking back on it now – an ice age ago – I feel a rush of weltschmerz and nostalgia. The girl's name was Marlene Beliveau. She was related to Jean Beliveau of the Montreal Canadiens. They were second cousins. Their kinship gave Marlene a kind of celebrity status. Not that she lacked popularity, for she was intelligent and very pretty, with shoulder-length blonde hair, gray eyes, and a smooth wholesome complexion that enhanced the gracefulness of her slender physique. Her only flaw, if such it can be called, was her indifference to Jean Beliveau and hockey. More than anything, I think she was amused by the fuss teenage boys made over her surname. Sports-minded as I was, I found her indifference perplexing. I suppose there was a certain snobbishness in her attitude. Whenever I asked her a question about Jean Beliveau, she would sigh, or toss her head haughtily and mention some vague family matter. It was for that reason I began talking to her about movies and music and school. The fact I was a goalie for a local hockey team didn't interest her at all.

Marlene's parents were from Quebec. They moved to Windsor, Ontario when Marlene was seven. Marlene spoke French at home. We were the same age. She was a sophomore at a Catholic high school for girls. I was only

a freshman – a fact I concealed from her. I went to a
Basilian-run high school for boys.

Except for sports, there were not many social activities for boys my age – the awkward age. Nor were there
opportunities to meet girls. The C.Y.O. (Catholic Youth
Organization) held Sunday night dances in the spacious
basement of Immaculate Conception Church. I had gone
there once or twice. The dances were low-keyed, orderly
gatherings, supervised by a priest. Rock 'n' roll was just
coming into its own, and Elvis Presley would soon be king.
The C.Y.O. played the safe, clean music of Perry Como,
Doris Day, Pat Boone and their ilk. The dancing was stiff-
hipped, patterned on specific rhythms; only certain moves
allowed, and boy leads girl. There was no free-style dancing or touching of bodies. The girls mostly danced the
1950s' version of the jitterbug with one another. The boys
– either wallflowers or given to posturing and showing
off – stood in small groups around the dance floor, eyeing
the girls and hoping to be noticed. Interaction between
the sexes was tentative, nervous, and blundering. However, some of the teens were real cool, like 17-year-old
Bob Gardner. He sported a duck's-ass haircut, affected
James Dean mannerisms, and was a star basketball player
at my high school.

At one of those C.Y.O. dances, in late November, I met
Marlene. My dancing experience was negligible; but when
I saw her standing with two other girls on the sidelines, I
walked over and asked her for a dance. The first record
we slow-danced to was "Earth Angel," by the Crew-Cuts.
Then we did a holding-hands fast dance to Jim Lowe's
"The Green Door." For the first time dancing showed me
an accepted social form of the body that mixed both sexes,
as sports never did. And dancing with Marlene made me
aware of my body in ways that sports never did.

In early adolescence, when the bloom of puberty is fresh as the dew on a rabbit's nose, and when every living moment is new, the affection one feels for another of the opposite sex seems boundless. After meeting Marlene, I mooned around at home and at school in a dream. I didn't know what to do with my feelings for her. They became an imponderable burden. In the evenings, homework seldom finished, I would phone Marlene. Our talk was friendly, noncommittal. A typical conversation would run something like this:

"Do you want to go for a walk in the park?"

MARLENE: I can't go out now. I have a history test tomorrow.

"I just heard Elvis singing "Don't Be Cruel" on CKLW. What are you doing this Saturday?"

MARLENE: I don't know yet. My girlfriend and I might go to a movie.

"Would you like to go ice skating?"

MARLENE: When?

"On the weekend . . . in the evening."

MARLENE (after a pause): I'll let you know tomorrow. Call me then. Okay?

"Yeah, okay. Your cousin scored a hat trick last night – against the Red Wings."

MARLENE: *Scored what?*

Sometimes Marlene's mother answered the phone. *"Marlene n'est pas ici en ce moment."*

My grasp of grade-nine French was enough to double my disappointment.

Marlene was a mystery to me. There was an ambiguity about her that my naivete romanticized. I was always trying to outguess her. She was quiet and reserved, and religious. She attended Mass every Sunday. My faith was fickle. I had to watch my language with her. If I let slip some blasphemy (as I was wont to do), she would chide me for taking the Lord's name in vain. I once made the mistake of telling her that my uncles (on my father's side) taught me to swear in Italian when I was a child. I had intended to amuse her, but she was shocked. Of course I didn't tell her that when I was a grade-schooler I used to steal prayer books from churches.

"French-Canadian chicks got hot pants." This remark was made by "Curly" Taylor during lunch period in our school cafeteria. Curly was a strapping 16-year-old sophomore who excelled in football. He was nicknamed Curly because of his short blond frizzy hair. He often joined me and a few of my jock classmates at lunch. Curly, who was brash to the point of arrogance, was always cracking dirty jokes and talking about girls in a slyly disparaging way. He seemed more experienced than most high-school seniors, and he crowed with an air of authority about "French ticklers," "hair pie," "lover's nuts," "stink-finger." We seldom disputed his opinions on sex. "A stiff cock has no conscience," he would say; and "Canuck broads moan for the bone. That's why they have so many kids." Curly's usual routine was to cup his armpit with his hand and pump his arm up and down so it sounded like his armpit was farting. Our dislike for each other was mutual. My enmity toward him stemmed from the fact he was forever taunting me about my sexual innocence in front of other boys. (I got even with him during an intramural football game. We were on opposing teams. Curly caught a lateral pass, galloped several yards with the ball, and was tackled by two players. There was a fumble, a scramble and, before the coach blew his whistle, I dived hard on Curly. My right knee fractured his left collarbone. He was carried off the field in a stretcher.)

Curly may not have been a brain at school, but he was a convincing liar and braggart.

Of course I wondered if Marlene had a secret boyfriend, if Marlene was a virgin. I was too proud, shy, and afraid to ask her. Yet those questions gnawed on my heart.

Marlene lived seven blocks away from me. One frosty night I walked past her house four times, hoping to catch a glimpse of her. A light was on in the front-room window. At one point a figure passed in front of the window. It might have been Marlene, but I wasn't sure. It could have been her mother; it could have been anybody.

On our first date – a Sunday evening in December – Marlene and I went ice skating at Lanspeary Park. The air was crisp, a light snow was falling, and Straussian waltzes were playing on the PA system. The outdoor rink was illuminated by eight overhead floodlights. A few dozen people were there. Marlene looked radiant in her white figure skates and bright red woolen scarf. We held hands as we skated counterclockwise around and around the rink. She was a good skater. She glided gracefully over the ice, and even executed some nifty figure eights. I began showing off by skating backwards, and fell on my ass. Marlene reached out her hand to help me up. I playfully pulled her down on top of me and started laughing. She was a bit discomposed, but then she laughed too. After an hour or so of skating, we stopped to rest. I bought each of us a cup of hot chocolate. Later, when I walked her home, I tried to steal a kiss. She jerked her head sideways, and my lips brushed her cheek. I made no further attempt. It was tacitly understood that nice girls didn't kiss on the first date.

The following Saturday I took Marlene to see *Love Me Tender*, starring Elvis Presley. The movie theatre was packed with teenagers. I slipped my arm around Marlene's shoulders. I could feel the soft warmth of her thigh through her skirt.

When the movie ended and we were leaving the theatre, someone called out my name. It was Curly Taylor. He was waving, shouldering his way through the crowd, toward us, a big grin on his face. Marlene paused. I grabbed hold of her hand and cut across a row of empty seats.

"Hey, wait up!" Curly shouted.

Curly caught up with us in the lobby. "Where's the fire?" he said, his eyes darting from me to Marlene. With Curly was some acne-faced guy I didn't know. We surged outside, then huddled on the sidewalk under the marquee. A light snow was falling.

"Ain't you gonna introduce me to your girlfriend?" Curly said, giving Marlene the once-over.

"Marlene . . . Curly," I said, impatient to leave.

"And he's Larry." Curly indicated his friend. "Moe couldn't make it." They both chuckled. "Man, that movie was dullsville. No rockin' an' rollin'."

"I liked it," said Marlene.

"Yeah? Well, whatever." Curly shrugged. "Hey, what say we all go somewhere for a pizza. I got wheels."

"Some other time," I said.

"C'mon, a little piece never hurt anyone," Curly said, giving me an elbow and a grin. His friend sniggered.

"We have to go," I said.

"What about you, Arlene?" said Curly.

"It's Marlene. No thank-you," she said.

"How come all you frosh are so square?" Curly said mockingly.

Marlene frowned. "What makes you think I'm a frosh?"

"Well, ain't you? *He is*." Curly nodded toward me. My heart sank. Marlene shot me a questioning look.

"I happen to be in grade ten," she told Curly.

"Where?"

"Saint Mary's Academy."

Surprised, Curly said; "Ain't that a school for girls who wanna be nuns?"

"A common misconception," she said. Her answer sounded rehearsed.

"Well, pardon my grammar," Curly smirked.

"Ah-hoore!" the boy coughed. The crude inflection was unmistakable.

"We have to go, Curly." I gave Marlene a little nudge.

Curly shrugged. "Yeah, sure. Don't do anything I wouldn't do." He leered at Marlene, then he and his friend turned and walked away, laughing.

The encounter with Curly hurt my relationship with Marlene. The fact I was only in grade nine seemed an affront to her pride. She asked me why I hadn't told her the truth. It caused a breach between us. Whenever I phoned her, she was unresponsive; her voice sounded flat. Nothing I said enthused her. She seemed to be busy all the time with schoolwork, girlfriends – excuses for avoiding me. I felt miserable.

On the third Sunday in Advent I went to the church Marlene attended, just so I could see her. She was there, with her mother – a tall slim woman with auburn hair. They even took Communion together. After the Mass I hung around outside the church. Marlene and I said hello to each other, but she didn't stop to talk with me. She acted very formal and proper. As soon as I got home, I phoned her and asked if she wanted to go for a walk in Willistead Park. In wintertime the park, with its tall trees, wrought-iron fence, Tudoresque manor and coach house, looked like a Currier and Ives Christmas card. "I'm going with my mother to a shower this afternoon," she said. "And I have to get ready." I began to think that girls lived a more secretive life than boys.

At school, Curly bugged me about Marlene. "Gettin' any nooky from that cockteaser?" he'd smirk. I tried to act hip, but he wasn't fooled. All his boastful yapping about sex got on my nerves. I didn't know enough about girls and sex to tease him back. "Go play with yourself," I'd sneer at him. "At least I got something to play with," he'd retort. It amazed me that despite the antagonism between us, we never came to blows. He would provoke me just so far, and then back off. Even when I visited him in the hospital (out of guilt, not regret), he succeeded in irritating me. Perhaps he thought I was there to gloat over his broken collarbone. As much as I denied injuring him on purpose, he did not believe me.

With Christmas holidays approaching, I looked forward to making up with Marlene. The ambiguous ardors of what is called "puppy love" had me in a spin. Being in love – puppy or otherwise – seemed like some form of self-punishment. Love was a destructive artifice, and hard to bear, especially if your love wasn't reciprocated. There were no hard-and-fast rules for love. Love was highly fugitive. Of course I didn't know that at fifteen.

Imagine my disappointment when Marlene informed me that she was going to Trois-Rivieres, Quebec for Christmas – where she and her parents and her younger brother went every Christmas. I felt betrayed, lost, alone. I was envious, too. The farthest I'd ever been was Niagara Falls. To console myself, I made her promise to get Jean Beliveau's autograph for me.

Marlene was true to her word. We were in the Harmony Grill, on Ottawa Street, eating French fries with gravy. She handed me a white envelope. "Open it," she said. Inside the envelope was a Christmas card: the three wise men on camels and a bright star overhead. The handwriting inside the card read: *Joyeux Noel 1956 – Jean Beliveau.* I was thrilled. I thanked her, I pressed her for details. I gave her a 45 record of "Earth Angel." She was touched by my gift but seemed reluctant to accept it. I sensed a certain distance between us, which I couldn't quite define. It was as if her trip to Quebec had changed her in some way. She looked so happy, she seemed so mature. She burbled about the wonderful time she'd had there, and said she wanted to move back to Quebec after she graduated from high school. I didn't know what to say. I was listening to her with my heart.

When classes resumed in early January, Marlene and I already seemed to be strangers to each other. Our conversations on the phone grew more and more desultory. For a while, movies and hockey distracted me.

The teachers at my high school were Basilian priests and habited scholastics. Besides the usual courses of study, the curriculum included Religious Knowledge. R.K. we called it. Our R.K. teacher was the Reverend Father Whyte. Each schoolday, before we began our lessons, Father Whyte impressed on our young minds two platitudes: *"Religious knowledge is the highest form of knowledge"*; and *"If you bear your cross willingly, it will bear you."* Sometimes he would call on one of us to parrot obediently what he expected us to say.

Father Whyte was a balding man in his late thirties, of medium height and slender build. He was humorless, finicky, pedantic, and excessively neat. Dirty hands were a source of real concern to him. His own hands were small, smooth and slender, like a woman's. They were hands that had never known a callous. He was forever wiping them of chalk dust and imaginary grime. Even the way he held a book in his left hand, delicately turning the pages with the fingertips of the other, gave us the impression he was fearful of picking up germs. He became very annoyed if he caught anyone dog-earing or annotating a textbook.

Our first day back in school Father Whyte reminded us that New Year's Day was also the Feast of the Circumcision of Jesus. "On the day he was circumcised," said Father Whyte, "he received the name of Jesus – the same name which had been appointed him by the angel Gabriel before he was conceived." His mention of circumcision provoked some snickering among us. He certainly had our attention. We spent the entire period discussing the mystery of virgin birth, and the fact that circumcision was a sacrament in the Old Testament.

For the next few days Father Whyte dwelt on the subject of circumcision. He read us several chapters from the Epistle of St. Paul the Apostle to the Romans about the knowledge of sin, about the flesh and the spirit. I remember one verse in particular, because I asked Father Whyte a question concerning its meaning. The verse was: "Circumcision is that of the heart, in the spirit, and not in the letter; whose praise is not of men, but of God." I forget his answer, but his harping on circumcision became a locker room joke.

It was only natural that those of us who played sports, wore jockstraps, and showered together became more conscious of one another's penises. In the locker room, Curly Taylor was in his element. Curly, who was uncircumcised, extolled the merits and advantages of having a foreskin. He rattled off at least a dozen crude reasons why girls preferred it uncut. I was one of the circumcised. Uncut or not, a big prick was still a big prick.

The outcome of all this banter and nonsense proved unsettling to Curly. It was Father Whyte's use of a strange-sounding word in class that caused Curly no end of indignation. Curly learned of the word and its meaning from one of my jock buddies. The word was *smegma*.

One day in early February I saw Marlene at Kresge's department store. I was standing two merchandise counters away from her. She was with some guy. He was taller than me and looked about two years older. They were standing close together, talking and laughing. I swallowed hard and slunk out of the store.

One day in early February Father Whyte took me aside and said: "I'd like to see you in my classroom after school."

A sudden misgiving chilled me. I looked at him. "Is there something wrong, Father?"

"No, no – nothing at all." He half-smiled to reassure me. "Just a small religious matter." He half-smiled again and walked away.

Later, when I approached Father Whyte's room, the door was closed. The long hallway was quiet and empty save for a few students rummaging in their lockers. I knocked on the door and it was opened almost at once.

"Come in," Father Whyte said, closing the door behind me. It was apparent he'd been pacing the floor. He seemed fidgety, expectant. He glanced at the clock on the wall. "You may take off your coat."

I removed my coat and laid it on one of the desks. I felt uneasy. I wondered how long the "small religious matter" would take. "What'd you want to see me about, Father?" I asked, trying to appear nonchalant.

He motioned me to sit down, clasped his slender hands and said: "Well, I've been going over your marks and test papers, and I can see a gradual improvement in your work.

Your attendance in class is good; but your work habits could do with a little more discipline. You seem easily distracted . . ." He fixed his eyes on me.

"I always hand in my homework on time," I said defensively.

"Yes, you're very punctual," he said, unclasping his hands. "However, it's not simply a matter of finishing your assignments on time." He cleared his throat and began to pace back and forth as he spoke. "Religious knowledge is a *commitment*. It's a special commitment to God – and to the service of things that are sacred. To acquire religious knowledge, a knowledge of your own body is important." He stopped pacing and looked at me. "Do you understand what I'm saying?"

"I'm not sure, Father," I replied, puzzled.

"What I'm trying to say is that your body should serve to glorify the Spirit. Unlike your soul, which is immortal, your body is the word made flesh, as the Gospel of Saint John tells us. Your body is a temple of the Holy Ghost." He paused, then continued. "A few weeks ago, when I was talking about the circumcision of Jesus, you asked me a question – a very sensible question – but I don't think you grasped the full import of my answer. Do you remember what I said?"

"Er, something about sin . . . righteousness . . ." I muttered uncertainly. I had no idea what he was driving at.

"Well, yes, that's partly correct," he said, and half-smiled. "When I spoke of the circumcised heart, I was using a figure of speech. The circumcised heart is a heart open to God's command and obedient to him, not closed and stubborn. Now do you understand?"

"Yes, I think so."

"Good. It's not just the spiritual circumcision of the heart, but one that springs from the Spirit of Christ himself. Circumcision is a symbol of faith and purification. Now . . . the question I must ask you is: *Are you circumcised?*"

I was stunned. I merely nodded. On the wall was a large round picture of the *Agnus Dei*. I gazed blankly at the haloed white lamb bearing a bannered cross. In my mind flashed an image of Marlene ice skating at Lanspeary Park.

"Well . . ." he said, then paused for a moment. "If you would please stand up, so we can have a look. A clean heart isn't closed and stubborn."

I stood up. He looked at me intently. Waiting.

In my innocence and nervous confusion I unzipped my fly and pulled out my penis.

"Yes," he murmured. His small slender hand reached for my penis. He began fondling it, explaining with clinical matter-of-factness how an uncircumcised penis looked, and showing me. I stood there as if paralyzed, feeling nothing. After a minute or so, he suddenly stopped. He seemed disappointed. I zipped up my fly. I felt awkward. He fished in his pocket and handed me a black rosary. "This is for you," he said. "It's been blessed."

"I've got one," I mumbled. My refusal of the rosary disconcerted him. He gave me a worried, searching look.

"This religious exercise need only concern us . . . priest and pupil," he said gravely. "Is that understood?"

I nodded.

He made the sign of the cross. "You may go now," he said.

A few days later I confided the incident, without mentioning certain details, to my mother. She was appalled and angry at the same time. "We'd better not tell your father," she said. "He'd have a fit." My father was an agnostic, and he loathed priests. Had I told him, he would have gone to my school and given Father Whyte a beating. My mother and I did not discuss the matter again. It was too shameful.

Nor did I mention it to my friends.

Yet I could not help wondering if I was the only boy whose penis Father Whyte examined. Were there others? Who knows? I felt unclean. It was as though my heart had been darkened by the knowledge of sin through the iniquity of a priest who, in the name of religion, had cast a light on sin.

BET I CAN SCARE YOU

In my youth there was a not-so-innocent game called *Bet I can scare you*. The game was played indoors, usually at night, by two players – the scarer who attempted by suggestion and ingenuity to scare the other player who, if frightened, had to holler *SCARY!* as an admission of defeat. The scarer had only thirty minutes to effect a successful fright. Touching with the hands or with any hand-held object was forbidden. The scare had to be much greater than any resistance to it. Anticipation and surprise were crucial factors in what was primarily a contest of wills. If the scarer failed, he or she had to pay five dollars to the other player, or vice versa. Although not as popular as charades and spin the bottle, *Bet I can scare you* was challenging, unpredictable and, as you shall see, sometimes disturbingly frightening.

Fifteen-year-old Randy Richardson prided himself upon his skill as a scarer, even bragged about it. Randy once confided to me that he spent hours dreaming up different ways to scare people. The truth was he took a perverse pleasure in scaring people. I suppose it made him feel invincible, gave him a sense of worth, a feeling of power and superiority over his peers and high-school classmates. I knew his tricks too well for him to frighten me.

Randy's good looks belied a devilish personality. Had his face been deformed by a harelip, or had he been physically repugnant in some way, then it would have seemed congruent with his proclivity for morbid fancies. Yet it was precisely this paradox which made him attractive to others. In the high-school yearbook photo of our class, Randy is standing beside me in the back row. He has a smirk on his face. In the "Class News" of that yearbook, the caption beside his name reads: *"Bet I can scare you."*

In physical size, Randy was indistinguishable from other boys his age. He had a high forehead and light brown hair. He was always well-groomed and favored pink dress shirts and black trousers. Four things struck me about him: his cold gray eyes, his glib use of big words, his addiction to Pride of Arabia instant coffee, and a killer smile that showed a row of perfect teeth.

Randy was fond of practical jokes, of solving puzzles and deciphering cryptograms. He was moody, egocentric, self-dramatizing, fiercely competitive about getting his own way, and sociable only with those over whom he could exert control. He was an avid reader of books on sorcery, and interested in hypnosis, psychokinesis, telepathy. He really believed that thinking hard enough about an occurrence could somehow bring it about. He kept a life-sized plastic skeleton of a human in his basement closet. Real or imagined fear fascinated him, especially people's phobias. If someone was, say, coimetrophobic – afraid of cemeteries – as was my 14-year-old cousin Linda, Randy was curious to know why. Ironically, he too had a phobia, one I shared with him. Chilopodophobia. We also shared a strong liking for Edgar Allan Poe.

Randy lived a block away from me, with his mother – a working woman – in the lower apartment of a red brick duplex that always looked dark because of the large maple tree in their front yard.

Randy was eleven when his father deserted him and his mother. Although Randy was an only child, he and his father had never been close. He used to fear his father's morose drunkenness and bad temper. For almost a year following his father's desertion, Randy would waken during the night and steal into his mother's bed. His mother had a difficult time breaking him of this habit, with the result that he became possessive and demanding of her, and irrationally jealous of her occasional male friends. One evening Randy removed the rubber nozzle from a bottle of liquid glue, and emptied the bottle into her boyfriend's galoshes. Another time he put two live black beetles into her lidded sugar bowl. Playing pranks on his mother became a pattern with Randy whenever she did something that displeased him. Accusations and quarrels flared up between them; but Randy always managed to get the upper hand. He knew how to manipulate his mother's weaknesses. Because she was docile and vacillating by nature, he exploited her. More often than not she granted him his wishes and yielded to his demands – perhaps out of her feelings of guilt and inadequacy. In short, she spoiled him. When she gave him a chemistry set for his thirteenth birthday and cautioned him to play with it in the basement, he carelessly ignited a flammable substance and burned a saucer-sized hole in the living room rug. Her day job took up most of her time. Randy was left to the guidance of his own will. He was unsupervised, and his actions frequently got him into trouble with his teachers. His mother lamented the fact that his willfulness wasn't subjected to very much discipline at school, yet she herself seemed uncertain how to impose it. Withholding his weekly allowance proved futile. After a time she stopped inviting friends to her apartment. Going to parties or to the movies also created problems for her. Randy would sulk or resort to insults, tell her she was "getting fat" or that she was "ugly." His disrespect hurt her. Sometimes she gave him the silent treatment. If criticism unhinged Randy, be-

ing ignored by his mother not only aggravated his insecu-
rity but gave him nightmares. Routinely they would embrace and make up.

I remember the first time Randy and I got into mischief together. It was shortly after his father vanished.
While walking along a dirt alley, we spied a few bushels of
empty wine and whisky bottles beside someone's back
porch. Certain that nobody was home, we climbed over
the fence. Each of us gathered up an armful of bottles and
began smashing them on the street, in front of the house.
A police car soon appeared. Randy escaped through a
backyard. I panicked and ran home. The police followed
me in their cruiser. Unbeknownst to us, the house was a
blind pig. We had done the cops a favor.

Halloween was made for boys like Randy. On Halloween he felt free to do whatever he liked. He prepared for
the event a week in advance, and his excitement didn't
wear off till a week after. One Halloween was mischie-
vously memorable. Randy wore a werewolf mask and his
mother's old fox-fur neckpiece. He shattered a neighbor's
kitchen window with an apple; punctured the tires of a
car with an ice pick; pulled down the handle of a fire alarm
box; and kept putting stones inside my cousin Linda's shopping bag of goodies when she wasn't looking. Some chubby
kid in a Superman costume had climbed up onto the roof
of a garage that faced the street. Randy began coaxing the
boy to jump, trying to convince him that his cape would
function as a parachute and slow the speed of his fall.
Meanwhile a motley band of ghosts, witches, pirates and
assorted monsters had gathered round to watch. The boy
jumped and broke his ankle.

When Randy was in grade eight, his class went on a
field trip to Yawkey Bush – a deciduous woodland outside
Windsor – to bird-watch, catch and observe insects, and
identify wild flowers. Randy and another boy stole away

from the group to seek more adventurous activities. Their teacher, who was also a scoutmaster, found them by a shallow creek. Randy and the other boy were both stripped to their underwear, whooping like savages, killing frogs by thwacking them with sticks. Randy was balancing in his hand a long cattail stem on which four frogs were skewered. For several minutes the angry teacher hid behind a sumac thicket and watched them. But his anger was thwarted by a sudden sensation of pleasure. He wanted to flog the half-naked boys with the scum-coated sticks they were killing frogs with. The image made him blush with shame and confusion. Still flustered, he approached the boys and ordered them to put on their clothes and rejoin the class. Seeing the teacher's nervous embarrassment, Randy gave him an impudent look, then muttered something to the other boy, who snickered slyly. The teacher turned and, without waiting for them to dress, stalked sullenly off.

So passed some of Randy's formative years. When I transferred from a Catholic all-boys high school to Patterson Collegiate and learned that Randy and I were going to be in the same sophomore class, I had mixed feelings. Although I liked Randy, and we sometimes hung out together, I didn't trust him. He was a bad influence. Yet it was hard to resist the force of his personality. He was close to me in expressiveness but alien in temperament. I played sports, he didn't. He considered high-school athletics "puerile" (his word) and a waste of time. He was a loner, and preferred movies to sock hops, reading Ellery Queen detective stories to going to parties. At school, he was a shit-disturber.

"Perverseness is one of the primitive impulses of the human heart," Randy once said to me, giving voice to a wisdom beyond his years. I later discovered he had quoted Poe. The reason he chose to quote that particular senti-

ment was significant, because it provided him with suffi-
cient self-justification for his misdeeds. It also shed some
light on a hidden recess of his character. I suppose his
waywardness was partly forced on him by circumstances
outside his range of understanding, plus the fact his mother
gave him certain privileges which he not only took for
granted but abused with impunity.

Girls were susceptible to Randy's good looks and killer
smile, his devil-may-care attitude. Yet he seemed indiffer-
ent to their flirtatious glances, their giggles, their teasing.
He liked my cousin Linda, though. Not in a sexual way;
no, he liked her unaffected simplicity and good-
naturedness. She was a perfect foil for him. The first time
he played *Bet I can scare you* with her, she didn't last ten
minutes. And he refused to take her five dollars. "Randy's
a real scharacter," she told me.

There was a tall hulking black boy in our class. His
name was Paul Talbot. Paul had hungry eyes for my cousin
Linda, but he was too shy to approach her directly; so he
kept pestering me to get him a date with her. When I
pointed out Paul to my cousin, and told her that he wanted
me to act as a go-between, she made a face, and said:
"Don't you dare!"

One day in the school cafeteria I told Randy about Paul's
secret passion for Linda. Randy was indignant. "I'll fix
that nigger's ass," he sneered.

The following day Randy took Paul aside, and said:
"Linda's really got the hots for you; but she doesn't want
her friends to start wagging their tongues. She'd like to
see you alone after school. At her house."

"Did she say that?" Paul asked suspiciously. "You ain't
puttin' me on?"

Randy kept a straight face. "Just go over to her house
and knock on the door. She'll be waiting for you. I'll give
you her address. Let me know when, and I'll tell her."

"Are you sure?" said Paul, his eyes brightening.

"What's little Oscar say?" said Randy, quoting one of Paul's pet slogans.

Paul smiled broadly. "Little Oscar says, 'I'm game.'"

"Right on! Oh, and don't forget a rubber," Randy winked roguishly.

"Yeah?" Paul's eyes bugged.

Randy nodded. "Yeah, if you don't mind taking a bath with your socks on."

"Thanks, man, I owe you one," Paul said, and slapped hands with Randy.

When Paul asked me if Randy's information was true, I was evasive. Of course I didn't inform my cousin.

Linda lived with her parents and our maternal grandparents in a two-storey frame house on an elm-lined street in an all-white, mostly Italian, neighborhood. Like Randy, she was an only child. Her parents were kind, honest, hardworking, religious and rigidly conventional. Randy had instructed Paul to go to my cousin's house around suppertime, when he knew her parents would be home. Paul, slicked up and cocksure, had gone.

To my dismay, Linda and her parents blamed me for the embarrassment I caused them. Strangely enough, Paul said nothing to Randy about the incident. He simply pretended Randy didn't exist. But he called me a "phony prick" and a "motherfucker." I saw the humiliation, hurt and bafflement in Paul's eyes. I felt ashamed.

"Wake up and die right," Randy chided me. "We taught numb-nuts a lesson, didn't we?"

The science lab at school was Randy's playground. Over the Bunsen burners, test tubes, petri dishes, and microscopes Randy hovered like a wizard enthralled yet reckless, butchering rather than dissecting frogs and earthworms, and conducting his own erratic experiments, for which he was sternly disciplined by the teacher. Yes, potassium reacted violently with water. "Let's have a conflagration just for the hell of it," Randy would whisper to me. He concocted a stink bomb that cleared the lab for a day.

Randy excelled in English. He outshone all the other students in Mr. Teternikov's English class. His compositions always got A's or A pluses. He was often asked to read his book reports aloud to the class. Vainly I tried to compete with him, but I lacked his extensive vocabulary, his way with words, his flair for conveying the grotesque, the morbid, the perverse. In that department he was matchless.

One of Randy's book reports made some girl nauseated. She tore out of the room, holding her hand to her mouth. Randy was so caught up in the gruesome scenes he was describing, that Mr. Teternikov had to tell him three times to stop reading. It was a graphic account of Poe's "The Pit and the Pendulum." Randy had introduced the tale by listing matter-of-factly a number of symptoms occasioned by the emotion of fear: dryness of the mouth and throat, nausea, difficulty in breathing, etc. In a solemn voice, he began correlating each of the symptoms with those suffered by the condemned prisoner in Poe's tale. It was a spellbinding performance. Mr. Teternikov was impressed, and praised Randy afterwards. Randy was a model student in Mr. Teternikov's class.

Every Saturday night, at eleven-thirty, WXYZ-TV broadcasted *Shock Theatre*. It showed horror classics like *Dracula*, *Frankenstein*, *The Black Cat*, *White Zombie*, *The Wolf Man*, *House of Horrors*. My cousin Linda, Randy and I, and our classmate Gerald Croley watched it at Randy's place. Randy likened *Shock Theatre* to a spiritual event. I thought he was exaggerating till he pointed out the word *ritual* in spiritual. In any case, *Shock Theatre* was our weekly ritual against the humdrum of schoolwork.

As soon as we got together, we'd order a large pizza, then light a black candle (Randy's idea); switch off all the lights, and gather in front of the 21-inch console TV. To the accompaniment of gloomy organ music, a human skull would appear on the black-and-white screen, a sepulchral voice off screen would say: *"Welcome to Shock Theatre – for the shock of your life,"* then laugh maniacally.

Randy could do a great impersonation of Bela Lugosi. He could even quote bits of dialogue from the horror movies we watched. He would ask us to identify the character with the quote, and to name the film.

"Do Boris Karloff in *The Raven*, when he begs Bela Lugosi to give him a face job," Croley would ask.

Randy, always glad to oblige, would contort his face. "'Maybe if a man looks ugly, he does ugly things.'"

Linda's favorite was Bela Lugosi rhapsodizing about the howling of wolves in *Dracula*. Randy would half-swoon: "'Listen to them. Children of the night. What music they make.'"

Randy thought the most diabolical quote of all was when Boris Karloff, the clubfooted torturer and executioner in *Tower of London*, pleads with Basil Rathbone – Duke of Gloucester – to allow him to kill as a soldier: "I've never killed in hot blood. It must be different, more . . . exciting."

Randy once bet Mr. Teternikov five dollars that he could recite "The Raven" by heart. Mr. Teternikov should have known better. I lost five dollars to Randy the same way.

"I told Teternikov that Bela Lugosi was buried in his Dracula cape," Randy said to me.

"What'd he say?"

Randy shrugged. "Nothing. He gave me a funny look."

The young married couple who lived next door to Randy brought home a dog one day; a full-grown, dark brindled boxer. For a week or two the dog was kept indoors at night. Then a doghouse was built in the couple's small, fenced-in backyard. The dog barked all night. It dirtied the yard with its excrement. The couple seldom cleaned up the mess. Randy regarded them as "low-class slobs." The dog barked at Randy whenever it saw him. Randy hated dogs. As a child, he'd been bitten on the shin by a neighbor's Tibetan spaniel.

The dog's barking affected Randy's sleep. He urged his mother to complain to the couple. "Tell 'em to strap a muzzle on their goddamn dog!" he grumbled. His mother promised, but she kept putting it off. In the meantime Randy seethed with resentment. When his mother finally admonished the man about his dog, she was told to mind her own business. Randy was furious. From that moment on Randy would disturb the dog if he saw it sleeping. When the couple wasn't home, he would bark at the dog and antagonize it. The dog would growl, bare its teeth in a vicious rage; strain violently at its chain or, if it was loose in the yard, snarl and slaver against the five-foot high wood fence, which Randy poked and banged at with a broken hockey stick. Whenever Randy came home late at night, the dog recognized his footsteps and growled.

One night it seemed the dog's barking would never stop. Randy lay awake in bed, his head churning with vindictive thoughts.

Next morning, a Saturday, Randy went to a grocery store and bought a large cleaning sponge and two cans of meatballs in tomato and meat sauce.

That evening, as it was turning dark, Randy slipped into the alley and skulked in the shadow of a garage behind the couple's house. The dog sensed his presence, and began barking. Randy whistled to it, then lobbed a meatball over the fence. The dog sniffed at the unexpected morsel, then wolfed it down. Randy whistled again, and tossed another meatball. The dog devoured it greedily. Randy ducked into the narrow, dim passageway that led to the side door of his apartment.

Randy repeated the feeding on Sunday evening. Four successive evenings he fed the dog only two meatballs. On the fifth evening he took the sponge, which was the size of a grapefruit, and wadded it up tightly with a piece of string. Then he soaked it thoroughly in the canned sauce till it resembled a meatball. Pleased with the likeness, he crept behind the garage and whistled to the dog. It barked twice, then stopped – listening, waiting. He tossed a real meatball to it, which it ate hungrily, then sniffed about for more. Randy whistled again, and lobbed the sauce-soaked sponge. The dog snapped it up instantly.

That night the dog moaned a little, but it did not bark.

When Randy came home from school the next day he saw the dog lying on the ground beside the doghouse. It was panting. He whistled once to the dog, but it just lay there.

During the next few days the dog became increasingly listless. Its stomach looked swollen. Gastric juice had loosened some of the string around the sponge. The dog whimpered a lot. Randy's mother remarked to him that the dog was probably sick. Randy said he hoped it didn't have rabies.

On a rainy Saturday morning the man next door took his ailing boxer to a veterinarian. He returned with the dog two hours later, looking very distraught. The dog had an intestinal infection. The couple was suspicious of Randy. Knowing they lacked real evidence, Randy was confident he wouldn't be found out.

Nine days after ingesting the sponge, the dog died. Randy was at school when it happened.

The partitioned, low-ceilinged, cement-floored basement contained a laundry room, a toilet stall, an unused coal bin, and a recreation room. The latter was Randy's hide-away, his sanctum. The door to it was always locked. (Randy had the only key.) Over the doorway was a sign, stenciled in ink, which read: ABANDON ALL HOPE YE WHO ENTER HERE. The room itself was furnished with an old, overstuffed, plum-colored sofa, an upholstered armchair, a floor lamp, a kitchen table and two chairs, and a threadbare throw rug. There was also a closet. The floor was covered with gray linoleum. On the walls were three red pentagrams, a cracked mirror, a print of "The Sabbatic Goat," by Eliphas Levi, and a framed photo-graphic print of Edgar Allan Poe – the one taken by Brady, in 1845. Except for the obvious occult effects and the slight smell of damp, it was a cozy room – the room where Randy played *Bet I can scare you*.

It was Friday night. Randy and I were sitting in his "un-holy lair," as he called it. He was drinking a glass of red wine and smoking a cigarette – indulgences he allowed himself occasionally. (He would also on occasion wash down three or four aspirin tablets with Coca-Cola – "to get a cheap high.") He seemed restless, irritable. We were talking about movies, rock 'n' roll, the physical attributes of certain girls at school – stuff like that – when, after a long pause, he blurted out: "Wu-kung Ching is the name of the centipede spirit."

"Huh? What are you talking about?" I looked at him, suspicious of his intent. I knew he wasn't drunk.

"The centipede spirit. Wu-kung Ching. He's one of the seven devils of Mount Mei."

"If you say so."

"I read it in a book," he said gravely.

"Kung ching? No thank-you, I'll have an egg roll." I chuckled. My joke annoyed him. I could see he was serious. I tried to feign interest. "Chinese mythology?"

"Of course. Knock-knock," he said, tapping his head with his knuckles. "The centipede is feared by the Chinese dragon – their lucky symbol."

I had no idea what he was driving at. Both of us had a phobia of centipedes. I figured he was trying to get a rise out of me. I decided to let him rave on. He lit another Black Cat cigarette, took a long, deliberate drag on it, and exhaled two perfect smoke rings. I watched them drift lazily in the air and then fade away.

"Ever wonder why you're afraid of centipedes?" he said.

"So are you."

He smiled slyly. "Some tropical centipedes are almost a foot long. And they're venomous. Just touching one, even if it's dead, can leave a scar on your hand . . ."

"You sound like an authority on 'em," I scoffed.

"They can capture and kill toads, lizards, even snakes. There's a big desert centipede in Arizona."

"Let's change the subject," I said.

"And there's the giant red and black Scolopendra of the Galapagos islands. Darwin discovered it. The fucker's two feet long! Its bite can paralyze a dog. Imagine being naked and locked up in a dungeon full of Scolopendras. Ugh! You wouldn't have a Chinaman's chance."

"Enough, goddamnit!"

"We must conquer our fear," he said, half smiling, gloating over my uneasiness. "Do you know how?" He paused for a moment. "By confronting it."

"I would if I could, but I can't, so I won't."

"The ones down here are only house centipedes." he said. "I've seen a few big ones though, in the coal bin." Suddenly he stared down at the floor beside my chair.

"What?"

He grimaced. "A centipede! It went under your chair."

I gave a start.

"Don't move!" He twisted around on the sofa, and groped behind a cushion. "BET I CAN SCARE YOU!" he shouted, and flipped a Mason jar at me. I caught the jar with both hands. Its cap was perforated by three nail holes. Inside the jar were bits of mossy bark – and a large centipede. He laughed. I flung the jar back at him. He bobbled it, and it slipped out of his hands and shattered on the floor. The centipede scurried away.

"GET IT!" he cried, springing to his feet. We both darted about the room, looking for the centipede. "THERE IT IS!" He stamped his foot once, twice, trying to squash it. The centipede disappeared through a crack in the baseboard.

"Fuck you, Randy!" I glared at him.

"Scared you, eh? It was Croley's idea. The bastard tried to scare me with it."

"I hope he scared the hell out of you."

"It's better to be scared than to be cursed," he said. "Let's clean up this mess."

"Your mess, not mine."

Grabbing a whisk broom and a dustpan, he began sweeping up the shards of glass. I didn't lift a finger. When he was finished, he sat down and lit a cigarette. There was a long silence.

"That yappy dog next door died today," he said suddenly.

Surprised, I looked at him. "How? What happened?"

He grinned. "I put a curse on it. It died a slow death." He got up, went over to his record player and slipped on an LP. Organ music filled the room.

"That stuff reminds me of a funeral," I said. "Play Elvis or Little Richard."

"You got Elvis on the brain." He lowered the volume. (It wasn't till many years later I recognized that organ music as Bach's *Toccata and Fugue in D Minor*.)

"Remember the night we blindfolded Linda, and drove to Windsor Grove. She got so scared, she wet her pants." He chuckled.

"That was a sick trick you played on her," I said. "With that freshly dug grave . . ."

"Look who's talking. You went along with it. I just wanted to cure her of her fear of graveyards."

"Yeah, till she got hysterical," I said.

"Hypnosis works sometimes. You should try it. A weak-willed person like you could be easily hypnotized."

"Who says I'm weak-willed?" I replied defensively.

"Your *horror*scope." He smirked. "Oh, certain people . . ."

"Bullshit. Who? Name one."

"Well . . . Croley, for starters."

"You're a liar. Croley wouldn't talk behind my back."

He smirked again. I should have known he was testing me, provoking me for his own amusement. He had a devious way of getting under one's skin, of bringing out the worst in people.

"Bet I can scare you," he said, then laughed. His laugh sounded forced, hollow.

"Get serious," I said. "Your time's up."

He glanced at his wristwatch. "Says who?"

"You really get a weird kick scaring people. Have you ever thought of seeing a shrink?"

His lips curled in a sneer. He gave me an icy stare. "I see things differently from you – from most people."

"Don't be so melodramatic."

"Sometimes you're dense as a forest." He paused, and then declared: *"I have a demon in my view."*

"And I'm a vampire," I said with sarcasm. I figured it was time to make my exit.

"I killed that mutt next door."

"Yeah, you put a curse on it," I said mockingly.

"No, I really killed it!"

I felt a nervous chill.

In a voice husky with excitement he began telling me about the sponge and the meatballs, and about the clever way he had enticed the dog. His eyes shone as he spoke of these things. I listened to him with shocked disbelief. He boasted that during the past three months, in various neighborhoods, he had killed four other dogs the same way. He was watching me as if trying to gauge from my expression the effects of his words. He said the police were probably looking for him.

Disgust surged up in me. I knew Randy was capable of doing some crazy things; but this . . . this was *evil*. Of course the thought he might be lying flashed through my mind. It was the look on his face that convinced me he was telling the truth. It seemed as though he not only expected my sanction but expected me to holler *SCARY!* Yes, I was alarmed, dazed even, by the sudden realization he didn't know me at all. Our friendship had become complicity. I felt both contempt and pity for him.

"Why are you looking at me like that?" he said.

I stood up wearily. I wanted to go hone. The gloomy room, the organ music, the sound of his voice . . . I had the uneasy feeling he was using me.

"Where you going? It's early." He got up too, and followed me like a shadow to the door.

"You won't tell anyone – ?" he asked suddenly.

"Don't worry, Randy. I won't say a word."

"Promise?"

I nodded. I felt emotionally implicated, as though listening to his confession had made me an accomplice.

He smiled wanly. "That's my man," he said, and extended his hand.

I didn't want to shake his hand. But I did. Against my will.

WILD PITCH

Pitchers, like poets, are born not made.
Cy Young

On May 9, the year Mark McGwire of the St. Louis Cardinals hammered 70 home runs, I took the mound for the Rockies in a Men's Senior Baseball League exhibition game against the Rangers, at Scarboro Village Park, in Toronto. I was excited, I had butterflies; but the sound of my warm-up pitches striking the catcher's mitt exhilarated me and bolstered my shaky confidence. My mannerisms were those of a veteran pitcher by virtue of my age more than by my experience. I performed the ritual of rubbing up the baseball, landscaping the dirt on the mound with my spikes, picking up the resin bag, and then flinging it down in the dust. Before the lead-off batter came to the plate . . . before I went into my windup, I had an existential crisis. I realized with sudden horror that I had wasted the better part of my life by not having pursued a baseball career – at least a potential career which, for reasons that have never been clear to me, I had forsaken several decades ago. Where I really belonged was on the pitcher's mound. It was my throne.

I threw nothing but fastballs that day. I held the Rangers hitless and runless for the three allotted innings I pitched – striking out two and walking two. In the dugout some of my teammates – guys I hardly knew, who hardly knew me – said: "Good pitchin' . . . Nice work . . . That's the way." My first time up at bat I swung at a slow curve. The ball glanced off the handle of my bat and tore the skin on the middle knuckle of my right index finger. My finger had to be bandaged. For a few days after that game my left hip was stiff and sore (probably from the kick and stride of my pitching motion). But my right arm felt strong, supple as a whip. I felt I could pitch forever, like Satchel Paige.

If memory is the only thing one can call truly one's own, then I could link up with memory and recapture my youth by playing baseball again. I could "piece together the past and the future," as T.S. Eliot said in his *Four Quartets*. I could fulfill my early promise. Such was my private delusion. I was 56 years old; out of shape, overweight, with a slight paunch – but healthy, determined, and very happy I had come back.

I think often about that day. And about that season, too. The details are vivid and live vividly in my mind. Seeing myself in a baseball uniform; wearing a used pair of Mizuno baseball shoes (low-cuts, the spikes rubberized) which I bought for only $12 at a Play It Again Sports store. My cap has a black crown, a gold *R* and a purple bill. Royal colors. My pants are gray polyester. My short-sleeved, three-button, mesh shirt is purple, and the word *Rockies* is scripted in white and outlined in gold across the front of it. On the back of my shirt is *16* in large block numerals. My brown Rawlings glove, with its "basket-web" and "deep well pocket" – a Fernando Valenzuela model – is old yet still serviceable.

The desire to play baseball again or, rather, to pitch again was always in the back of my mind. Pitching was what I enjoyed most about baseball. I loved to pitch. It was the first thing in my life that I could do well and others couldn't. The game itself was incidental, secondary to my pitching. I couldn't hit worth a damn, nor could I play skillfully in the field. I was solely a pitcher. Throwing a baseball felt like the most natural thing in the world. As a boy, I believed the way you threw a ball (I mean the actual rhythm that propelled it through the air by the motion of your hand, arm, and body – instead of merely flipping the ball) was an accurate indicator of your character. I suppose something in me still believes that. (Girls throw like girls. Some boys throw like girls.) I remember my father once telling me that human evolution began the first time some caveman picked up a stone in self-defense and threw it another caveman, thus avoiding hand-to-hand combat and possible injury to himself.

In the early spring of 1998 I was gripped by baseball fever. Its onset precipitated my decision to do something about it. I was tired of being a poet, weary of inspecting the lyre. I had been a poet too long. 31 years. I had published nine books of poetry, including a book of children's verse, plus three poetry chapbooks. I had edited, with an introduction, the collected poems of a Canadian poet. A one-act play of mine had been produced in Montreal. My poems had appeared in dozens of magazines and anthologies. I had conducted poetry workshops at several community colleges; given poetry readings all over Canada, and in Detroit, Boston, New Orleans, Seattle. I had reviewed hundreds of books of poetry and fiction; received many writing grants. I had won a literary prize for my poetry. My friends and acquaintances knew me as a poet. Readers of poetry were familiar with my name. For three decades, poetry was not only my purpose but my passion. I was a prisoner of poetry. An 8 ½" by 11" sheet of lined paper was the barred window through which I peeped out, trying to render a poetic image of reality. Now I wanted out of my paper prison. I wanted to grip a baseball instead of a ball-point pen.

In my journal I once wrote: "I threw away my talent for pitching a baseball when I picked up a pen to write a poem." In the same journal was another entry, dated:

"October 16, 1997. While out for a late afternoon walk, I saw a seagull standing on the pitcher's mound at Christie Pits." I regarded the sighting as a good omen because I once wrote a poem about Vancouver fog and middle-aged angst, which contained the line: *My only beacon is a seagull*. Strange that I never wrote a baseball poem.

I had no connections in amateur baseball. I knew about the Intercounty Baseball League and the Toronto Maple Leaf Baseball Club. I also knew my age was against me. If I was going to pitch again, I would have to start from scratch. So I began making phone calls. I phoned Toronto Parks and Recreation. But I got nowhere. Should I put an ad in the newspaper? *Have balls, will pitch*. Who wants a 56-year-old pitcher? Was I really over the hill? Finally, in desperation, I dialed the home telephone number of Jack Sunday, the owner and president of the Toronto Maple Leaf Baseball Club. I told him my name, I explained my situation, and then I asked him straightaway about the possibility of pitching batting practice for the Leafs. He must have thought I was some crank. When I mentioned my age (I lied that I was only 49), he said: "Are you crazy?" I lied, too, about having pitched winter ball in Mexico the previous year – assuming, hoping he would be impressed. He merely hemmed and hawed.

"What does your wife say about all this?" he asked in a patronizing tone.

I thought his question irrelevant. "I'm divorced," I said, which was true.

That seemed to stump him. There was a brief silence. "I'll have to speak with the team's manager. I'll get back to you," he promised, without asking for my phone number. (I gave him my number twice.) "Yeah. I'll get back to you," he said flatly. He sounded impatient to get off the phone.

I was less than hopeful. The tone of his voice was discouraging and unfriendly. At least he could have tried to be more helpful. Needless to say I never heard from him.

I continued to make inquiries until my persistence paid off. There was an amateur baseball league for men over 30 – in Scarborough, a dreary suburb called locally "Scarberia." The league consisted of four teams: Marlins, Phillies, Rangers, and Rockies. Games would be played every Saturday at Neilson Park, from mid-May until mid-September. Overjoyed, I signed up at once. I shaved five years from my age, and I proudly informed the league's director that I was a right-handed pitcher. I was assigned to the Rockies. No *I-coulda-been-a-contender* syndrome for me. Now I was a contender.

I have never been able to write in the summertime. Too much humidity and temptation. Besides, there's something perverse and unhealthy about sitting at a desk, trying to write poetry, when the weather is beautiful. I'm a foul-weather poet.

I knew I was out of shape. I weighed 200 pounds. I smoked a pack of cigarettes a day. So I started exercising daily. I cut down on pasta. I bought a pair of hand-grips, which I squeezed till my forearms bulged, etched with veins. Twice a week I worked up a sweat running windsprints in a nearby park. To strengthen my back muscles, I did countless sit-ups. During the week I had no one to play catch with. For a half hour each day I threw a rubber ball against the cement wall of a school in my neighborhood. Passers-by sometimes stopped to gawk at me – an adult playing alone with a ball. At night, in my room, in front of the mirror on the wall, I practised my pitching motion in pantomime. A pitcher's motion should have rhythm. It's like a kind of dance: pump, kick, stride, release, follow-through. The technique of pitching began to obsess me. So did my age.

To find out the average age of professional pitchers when they hung up their spikes, I consulted the *Baseball Encyclopedia*. Very few were still active at 40. In fact, their pitching careers were kaput by 35. Besides the ageless Satchel Paige, there were three notable exceptions. Hoyt Wilhem pitched till he was 49. Nolan Ryan till he was 46. And Warren Spahn till he was 44. A pitcher's career was short. Sandy Koufax was only 30 years old when he quit. Of course all those facts depressed me. What the hell was I trying to prove by pitching at my age? I didn't want to think about it. My friends thought I was crazy, or just going through a phase. "I wish I had a twenty-year-old arm," I said to Ted Plantos, a poet-friend my age. "Wouldn't you rather have a twenty-year-old girl on your fifty-six-year-old arm?" he said. Another friend suggested I seek psychiatric help.

It took me an hour and a half by subway and bus to get to Neilson Park. Although it had lights for night games, the ball park itself was so-so. The outfield was enclosed by a 10-foot high chain link fence. Dusty grass outlined the infield. The pitcher's mound looked like a sand trap.

Most of the players on our team (there were 15 of us weekend warriors) were in their middle to late thirties. A few were in their early to mid forties. Only one other player was in my age bracket. He was a pitcher, too: a right-hander who threw sidearm. He had a good curve, but his fastball wouldn't have broken a pane of glass.

My teammates were jock types, strangers to me. I never got to know their last names, though three of them were named Mike. Except for baseball we had nothing in common. They all had gainful occupations. Our coach was a graphic designer; our catcher worked for the Humane Society; our first baseman was an auto mechanic; our center fielder sold real estate. Had my teammates known I was a poet, there would have been raised eyebrows. I told them I was a free-lance writer. I think they considered me something of an oddball. In any case, I wasn't playing baseball to win a personality contest.

The league supplied the teams with aluminum baseball bats – to save money, I guess. Unlike the Louisville Slugger, an aluminum bat was lighter and didn't break. For the sake of tradition, I bought a Louisville Slugger – a Cal Ripken Jr. model. The 35-inch bat didn't improve my batting average.

Because I had pitched so well in the exhibition outing, I started the opening game of the season against the Phillies. Again I relied on my four-seam fastball. I threw with a three-quarters overhand motion, which made the ball's 108 stitches bite the air. I lasted only two innings before getting a sharp pain in my lower back. It was difficult to stride and follow through properly. I kept landing on my left heel or on a stiff left leg. I didn't give up any runs, but I was disappointed my back gave out. As if that pain wasn't enough, I got hit on my left forearm by a pitch my first time at bat. The imprint of the ball's stitching on my skin looked like the fossil of a centipede. We beat the Phillies 7-4.

My second appearance was a start against the Marlins. I worked four innings and allowed six runs, two of them unearned. We lost 8-6. After the game I kept getting lower back muscle spasms. The next day I couldn't stand upright. I could hardly move. I couldn't even sit comfortably in an easy chair. I tried extra-strength Robaxacet caplets, tiger balm, herbal tea, whisky. Nothing helped.

A friend's wife advised me to see a chiropractor she knew. I was skeptical; but she swore this chiropractor could work miracles, and besides the first consultation was free.

The chiropractor's office was on an upscale block in Cabbagetown. There was standing room only in the waiting room. I regarded that as a good sign, and told the receptionist I was stepping outside for a smoke. When it finally came my turn, the chiropractor asked me a few questions. He looked fiftyish, and was tall, portly, suntanned. His hair was dyed chestnut brown. He had on a Hawaiian shirt unbuttoned halfway down his hairy chest, and three thin gold chains around his neck. He was also sporting a Rolex wristwatch. He could have passed for a lounge lizard. He asked me to lie down on a leather-upholstered bench. I removed my shirt, and lay prone. He began massaging my lower back with some kind of electrical device. "Electromyopercussion," he called it. I tried to count the syllables. His cell-phone chimed. He answered it. While he was chatting away, I suddenly felt the electrical device massaging my wallet. Annoyed, I told him so. The whole procedure was cursory to the point of being slapdash. I didn't make a second appointment.

I considered shiatsu, acupuncture; but my health care plan wouldn't cover the cost of those treatments, and I could not afford the latter. Dejected, I made an appointment to see a doctor in Family Medicine at Mount Sinai Hospital. When I told the doctor I was pitching in a hardball league, he shook his head in disbelief. He advised me it would be safer if I switched to slow-pitch. I nixed the idea. He prescribed Ibuprofen 400mg for me. I had to take one tablet three times a day. The tablets were bright orange and marvelously effective.

It wasn't until the first week of June that I pitched again. Three innings of middle relief. The game was a wipeout. The Phillies clobbered us 18-4. My back was okay; but my right elbow hurt.

The player who was the last out in a game had to lug our team's big canvas equipment bag to our coach's car parked about a hundred yards away from the dugout. The bag was cumbersome. It contained balls, bats, batting helmets, a catcher's mitt, mask, shin guards, and a chest protector. To compensate for my mediocre performance on the diamond, I often volunteered for that chore of bat boys. After each game, whether we won or lost, our coach treated us to a case of beer which he kept in a cooler in the trunk of his car. I would drink one or two beers. I found it difficult to join in the camaraderie among my teammates.

In the late 1960s, the pitcher's mound was lowered from 15 inches to 10 inches – obviously to give the hitters some advantage. A pitcher pushes off the rubber for momentum, bearing down on the batter. The 15-inch mound gave the pitcher more leverage to hurl the ball like a bullet. The dirt on the pitcher's mound at Neilson Park was loose and dusty. After two or three innings, the ground in front of the rubber was like a pothole. I had to stand almost on tiptoe with my right pivot foot, which made for an awkward stance that impaired my motion. When facing a left-handed hitter, I always stood with my pivot foot on the first base side of the rubber; and on the third base side of the rubber when pitching to a right-handed hitter. The pothole prevented me from using those angles in my release of the ball.

After my two failed starts, I mostly relieved, and often had to be relieved because of a sore arm. I couldn't pitch more than two innings without experiencing pain in my elbow and forearm. Yet one satisfactory incident stood out in my relief work. It was the bottom of the ninth, and our team was ahead 10-7. With two out and runners on second and third (a walk and an error), I fanned the Marlins' clean-up hitter with a shoulder-high fastball.

One Sunday morning I woke up and couldn't raise my right arm. My shoulder felt on fire. In a panic, I spent the day applying an ice pack to it. Even Ibuprofen couldn't alleviate the burning pain. When my lady friend saw my dejection, she commiserated, saying: "Why don't you play another position? Then you won't have to throw so much."

Two doctors examined my arm. One of them jokingly asked me if I was going to try out for the Blue Jays. The look on my doctor's face said *I told you so*. He filled out a rehabilitation medicine requisition. His diagnosis read: "Right shoulder supraspinatus tendinitis. Right biceps, triceps strain." He recommended physiotherapy – a word that made me feel like a cripple.

The physiotherapy clinic at the hospital had a two-month waiting list. So I went to a private clinic – one that specialized in sports injuries, like rotator cuff tendinitis.

Dr. Baida was a six-footer, like me, and he looked in good shape for a man in his middle sixties. He read my requisition. "Do you play tennis?" he said. When I explained how I had injured my arm, he frowned, and wagged his finger at me. "Who do you think you are – some young hotshot?"

"I'm having fun," I said, making a throwing motion.

"A guy your age should take up golf," he said.

I gave a little grimace. "No thanks."

"Well, if you want to play baseball, play in the outfield. If you keep on pitching, I can't rule out the possibility that you're risking permanent damage to your arm. What you have is RSI. Repetitive stress injury. It's an injury which results from using the same tissues over and over again, past their normal level of endurance. We have to treat the problem and not the symptom. The pain in your arm is only a symptom. The problem is pitching. You shouldn't be pitching."

His prognosis sounded like a death sentence. I lived for each Saturday's game. I was suddenly shocked into realizing that I wasn't even pitching against time. My time as a pitcher had ended years ago. Seeing my disappointment, he mentioned that he used to be a ballplayer; a third baseman. He told me that he once tried out for the Detroit Tigers at their spring training camp in Florida. This personal information made me feel better. At least he sympathized with my situation.

"What happened to your career?" I asked.

"Nothing," he said. "I went to university. I chose medicine over baseball."

"Any regrets?"

He searched me with a glance. "It was a long time ago. My prospects were slim."

"I regret giving up baseball," I said gravely. "It's my biggest regret." Then I mentioned how good my prospects had once been.

He smiled. "So you're making a comeback? You're not young anymore." He paused for a moment. "Just remember one thing. You can't fake what is physical."

I had physiotherapy twice a week: on Mondays, to revitalize my ailing arm, and on Fridays, to limber up for Saturday's game. The heat therapy, electrostimulation, vitamin B6, and arm exercises felt great. I was despondent though, in the grip of my baseball past. Poetry, which I had hitherto pursued with a passion, no longer seemed vital. It had been my *raison d'être*. To compose a poem, I needed artificial stimulants: tobacco, coffee, marijuana. To pitch a baseball, I needed physiotherapy. I had come full circle.

"The man who refuses to love what he loves dooms himself," wrote Vincent van Gogh, in a letter to his brother. I knew what his insight meant, but I didn't care. If I couldn't pitch, then to hell with poetry. Hadn't T.S. Eliot called poetry "a mug's game"? He wrote: "It is my experience that towards middle age a man has three choices: to stop writing altogether, to repeat himself with perhaps an increasing skill of virtuosity, or by taking thought to adapt himself to middle age and find a different way of working."

You can't fake what is physical. Dr. Baida's words reverberated in my brain like Eliot's "fatalistic drum." Of course he was right. The body has its own wisdom. Unlike the intellect, the flesh doesn't lie. You can't fake hitting a home run. You can't fake pitching a fastball. Who does the mind play with when the body is ill? Neither pride nor stubbornness had a hand in my desire to pitch. I just wanted to pitch – for the joy and physical pleasure of pitching. And I did – gamely, despite the risk to my arm. Midway through the season I turned 57.

From July to the end of the season I pitched in only three games totaling 5 2/3 innings. I threw hard, but I was wild, I walked batters. (Too short a stride produces a high pitch; too long a stride produces a low pitch.) I fidgeted so much on the mound that my catcher said I'd make coffee nervous. I limited myself to two cigarettes a game. In one of those games my catcher kept signaling me to throw a curveball. I kept shaking off his sign. Exasperated, he removed his mask and waddled out to the mound. "You gotta mix it up, man!" he grumped. "The fucker's expectin' a fastball every time."

"Yeah, I know," I muttered irritably. I hadn't thrown a curveball in all the innings I'd pitched so far. I knew that throwing one would hurt my elbow. Besides, I wouldn't be able to get enough spin on a curve, nor control it. In the 85-degree heat, I was sweating like a packhorse.

I pitched three slow, weak curves in succession. The batter fouled two of them. On a full count I unloaded a waist-high fastball. He whacked it for a triple. I was so rattled that I walked the next two batters. Our coach relieved me with the bases loaded, one out, and the score tied 4-4. I walked off the mound and sat in the dugout. The frustration I felt was intense as my throbbing elbow. What had Dr. Baida called it? "Inflammation of the lateral epicondyle." I was learning a new language for which I had no metaphors.

By late August I no longer pitched. I was relegated to right field; put out to pasture. I played only a few innings each game, and mostly warmed the bench or warmed up the wanna-be relief pitchers. Sometimes my arm was so sore that I had to throw sidearm.

How I envied and admired young pitchers who threw smoke. *A strong, hard-throwing right-handed pitcher* was music to my ears when I was young. That was how my mentor Gene Dziadura – a minor-league infielder – described me to Chicago Cubs' scout Tony Lucadello. At 17, I could throw a baseball faster than anyone my age in Windsor, Ontario. At home or in the dugout I was always holding a ball with my various fastball grips because I believed it would strengthen the muscles and tendons in my right hand.

One night I came across the word *mortmain* in a book I was reading. The meaning of the word was unknown to me, so I looked it up in my big 13-pound *Webster's* dictionary. Literally the word means *dead hand.* However, the true significance of its definition startled me: *the influence of the past regarded as controlling or restricting the present*. Was I in the grip of a *dead hand*? Thinking that *mortmain* would be a good title for a poem, I suddenly realized the poet in me was still alive.

Memory is seeing who we are after what we were. I was lost in the half-life of memory; living in the past. My baseball past. I suppose only the past is *real* in the absolute sense that it has occurred. The future is only a concept that looms ghostly. The present is that fateful split second in which all action takes place. Memory, perception, expectation. Why does the human mind have the disturbing habit of willfully forgetting whatever in its past doesn't flatter or confirm its present point of view? With me it was just the opposite. The present wasn't living up to my past. It was merely adumbrating it.

Memories, images, fragments "of what is past, or passing, or to come." *I ate, drank, and slept baseball. I used to throw a mean spitter. I grunted every time I fired a fastball. On my way home from Wigle Park after a ball game, I always stopped at Peerless Dairy for a peanut-toffee sundae (the best in Canada), and scooped it up greedily with a long-handled spoon out of a tall tulip glass. I collected bubblegum baseball cards. In the 1950s, my favorite major-league pitchers were Bob Friend, Pittsburgh Pirates; Camilo Pascual, Washington Senators; Bob Turley, New York Yankees; Bob Porterfield, Washington Senators; Carl Erskine, Brooklyn Dodgers. Tony Lucadello, a scout for the Chicago Cubs, was impressed by my fastball. He said it "hopped," meaning it spun upward and slightly off center as it crossed the plate. Tony regarded me as a future prospect. He was the scout who signed Hall of Famer Ferguson Jenkins of Chatham, Ontario. I once pitched a no-hitter. I once struck out 16 in a seven-inning game. In 1958, I was the top pitcher (with a 6-1 record) in the "E" Division of the Mic Mac Baseball League. I once pitched two complete games in one day. I once . . . I was . . . I once was . . .*

My hardworking father never forgave me for giving up baseball. He felt I had let him down and shortchanged myself. "You can't earn a living writing poetry," he said. The truth is – I lacked ambition and self-discipline. Hence I was susceptible to influences – good and bad – that deflected me from the base path. My grade 10 English teacher, Tony Techko, was a good influence. He introduced me to the work of Fyodor Dostoevsky. "If you want to know all about humankind, read Dostoevsky," he said. After reading *Notes from the Underground*, I was never the same.

Books were my source of vicarious experience. Books also inspired me to experience life.

Girls and women were a big influence. They still are.

When I began writing and publishing poetry in my middle twenties, I didn't realize that the price I would have to pay for doing what I wanted to do was that I would *have to do it*. However, I knew that writing meant freedom, especially the freedom of being. If you can't be yourself, what's the point of being anything at all?

The last game before the play-offs (exactly four days after my tenth book of poems was published), I got busted on the back of my right hand by a curveball that didn't break. The pain dropped me to my knees. I had to leave the game.

My bruised and swollen hand was X-rayed. Luckily no bones were broken. Now I couldn't even grip a baseball, let alone throw one. I felt utterly defeated. I'm not superstitious, yet there were times when I thought my Muse was revenging herself on me for my continual neglect of her. She obviously wasn't a baseball fan. Was I making a Parnassus out of a pitcher's mound? Did I dare eat a Cracker Jack?

During the season I had missed three games because of injuries. Despite a cold and a purplish yellow bruise on my hand, I played right field in both games of the final doubleheader against the Marlins. At bat, I walked twice, grounded out, flied out, struck out, and lined a base hit. I even scored a run. Our team won both games – and the championship!

I finished the season with an 0-1 record and a 4.85 earned run average. I pitched 16 1/3 innings. I walked 15 batters and struck out 10.

In his book *Ball Four*, onetime New York Yankees' pitcher Jim Bouton wrote: "You spend a good piece of your life gripping a baseball, and in the end it turns out it was the other way around all the time."

One sunny afternoon in October a friend and I were playing catch. We were at Memorial Park in Windsor, Ontario. I was lobbing the ball, limbering up; relaxing, enjoying the sun's warm rays. Suddenly my friend crouched like a catcher and stuck up his glove. "Put something on it," he said.

I gripped the ball across the two narrow seams, wound up, and cut loose with a fastball. It spun upward and slightly to his right as he caught it.

"Ow, that stung!" he said, yanking his hand out of the glove.

I saw the trajectory of that pitch – a white blur – going on forever, from past to present, from the pitcher who might have been to the poet who once pitched, until it seemed suspended in time.

If there is such a thing as reincarnation, I hope I come back as a baseball pitcher.

OFF–OFF–BROADWAY

For three months Mike Simmons lived with the gnawing uncertainty that he may have killed a man. When he fled New York City on a Greyhound bus that muggy August night, he was numb from nervous exhaustion, appalled by what he had done, and fearful the police were looking for him. During the fourteen-hour bus ride to Detroit he slept fitfully, even though he had a seat to himself. In the morning, at the Greyhound station in Cleveland, he felt scruffy, and went to the rest room to freshen up. It was then he noticed dried blood encrusted on his leather watchband. After trying to scrape off the telltale scabs with his thumbnail, he removed the wristwatch and stuck it under some dirty clothes in his duffel bag. In the cafeteria, he wolfed down a western sandwich and drank two cups of coffee. The violent episode of the previous night seemed unreal as a B movie. It was as though he had wakened from a bad dream. The images of his brief stay in New York City assailed his mind with their luridness.

Mike Simmons was 20, slim, and of average height. He was educated yet unemployed, easygoing yet searching for something he lacked both the maturity and good judgment to define. Having no work-related skills, he toiled as a casual laborer whenever he was short of cash. For amusement he shot a fair game of pool and read mystery novels. For adventure he enjoyed hitchhiking to strange cities. One August morning in 1961, he decided to thumb his way to New York City via Niagara Falls. He had his duffel bag and $47 in his wallet.

New York City was like nothing Mike had ever seen. If this city was the top of the world, Mike felt as if he were at the bottom – anonymous and alone. It was evening when he wandered into Times Square, and he was dazed by the kaleidoscopic colors of neon signs, the vast crowds thronging the streets and spewing out of subways. Exhaust fumes from countless crawling cars hung in the humid air. Feeling lost, he drifted with the flow of human traffic – past porno shops, bars, strip joints, all-night movie houses, greasy spoons, massage parlors; among prostitutes, drug pushers, derelicts, winos, panhandlers, vagrants, and those who seemed to have abandoned even the semblance of human beings. Although it was mid-August, he noticed that most of the people looked stunted and pasty-complexioned. He was glad his face and arms were suntanned. It gave him a sense of identity. After drifting around Times Square for a few hours, he was no longer aware even of people, but of an insensible human mass. It suddenly occurred to him that he needed a place to sleep. He was tired, tense, distracted by the incessant tumult of sights and sounds.

Along each side of the main entrance to the Astor Hotel a number of young men loitered. They were mostly in their twenties. Mike reckoned they were hustlers; but he was surprised to see so many. He approached one of them and asked for directions to the nearest YMCA. At first the young hustler smiled, then he became suspicious, trying to size up Mike as a score or a wiseass. Mike explained his situation. The hustler gave him a funny look, then said: "There's a Y over on 34th. Where you from?"

"Detroit," Mike lied, reluctant to say – *Windsor, Ontario . . . you know? In Canada.* Just then the hustler fixed his attention on an older man who was lingering nearby. He nodded to Mike, and then went over to the man and exchanged a few words with him. They walked away together. Mike turned, then trudged down Broadway, wondering if the Y on 34th Street was east or west of Fifth Avenue.

That night, at the Sloane House YMCA, Mike was propositioned by a man from Texas. Mike was alone in the communal washroom, standing at a urinal, when a man shuffled in and used the urinal next to his. The man was wearing a blue bathrobe. He was short, stout, middle-aged. He glanced up and down at Mike. Annoyed, Mike shifted nervously. The man smiled. "Hell, don't mind me – it's a habit." With sly humor, the man said he was an inspector at a meat-packing plant in Houston. "I'm in town for a convention," he added. His breath smelled of whiskey. Mike shrugged, zipped up his fly, and turned to leave. The man spun around – his robe untied, and drawled: "Hey, if you're bored an' all, I got some girly mags an' a bottle of Jim Beam in my room." Mike mumbled: "Thanks anyway." The man stood there, holding his penis, disappointment clouding his face.

The next morning Mike checked out of the Y. Dollarwise it was either one more night at the Y or a decent meal. The day was hot. He roamed the streets of Midtown; browsed his way through an air-conditioned bookstore, and hung around Bryant Park, watching the weirdos. He wandered into the main reading room of the New York Public Library. Then he walked all the way to Central Park, where he relaxed on a bench and smoked three cigarettes. Nearby, a raggedy old black man was squatting outside a small hut made of scraps of plywood, cardboard, burlap, fiber glass, and some unrecognizable materials. Now and then the man would preach at passers-by.

Walking back to Times Square, Mike noticed that the same beat-up, black, tail-finned Cadillac he'd seen several hours ago was still there; and slumped over the steering wheel was the same heavyset black man. Mike wondered if the man was asleep or dead. Every few minutes a siren wailed somewhere.

By late afternoon Mike was so frazzled that he was functioning on impulse alone. Unable to decide his next move, he descended into the 42nd Street subway. He bought a token and boarded one of the graffiti-comic book-colored cars just for the sake of something to do – the sense of movement, of being swept along. The cars were often crowded, the stations noisy and dirty; but he felt relieved to ride under and over the streets of Manhattan and lose himself in the maze of tunnels. In the subway, he saw a bearded black man – barefoot and wild-eyed – frenziedly slashing the air with his fists, shouting over and over: "Hit me, muthafuckah, hit me!" He saw a fat, busty white woman with false eyelashes, wearing skintight pink slacks, scolding her child. The child looked unwashed and undernourished. He glimpsed a plaid sport jacket going down on a pair of Levi's in a doorless toilet stall that was crawling with cockroaches. He mostly saw ugliness.

It was evening when Mike got out at Washington Square. *So this is Grennwich Village*, he thought. Having read about the famed Village in novels, he felt for the first time he was on familiar ground. As he wandered around, the reality of gross commercialism gradually dispelled his romantic notions of the place. The fact he was alone and didn't know a soul made him wary, defensive. He bought a slice of pizza, and sat down on a bench to eat it. Presently a man strolled by, stopped, and said to him in a friendly tone: "The pizza is good, yes?"

"Huh? Yeah – excellent," said Mike.

The man smiled. "It is all right I sit here?"

Mike nodded. The man was in his thirties but boyish-looking, with a dancer's supple physique. "I am Mario," he said. He seemed courteous and not the least obtrusive, despite the alacrity with which he sat down and began chatting with Mike. He spoke with a slight foreign accent. Mike had the impression the man was lonely, and warmed to him right away. He learned that Mario was Italian, and that he worked as a draftsman. "In the Empire State Building," Mario said.

Impressed, Mike asked: "Which floor?"

"*Sessanta-nove*. Sixty-nine," Mario said, studying Mike's face for a moment. "On a clear day you can see fifty miles."

"Heights make me dizzy," said Mike. "I can't even climb a ladder."

When Mario realized Mike was homeless and not some street hustler, he suggested they go somewhere for a glass of wine. Sensing Mike's hesitation, he said: "You are my guest. I will pay."

They went to a café on Bleecker Street. The café was crowded and dimly lighted. Loud music was playing. Mike couldn't help noticing the café's patrons were mostly men. As he followed Mario to a table, he felt someone's hand slide lightly over his buttocks.

Mike's first glass of red wine made him tipsy. At Mario's urging, he drank a second glass while helping himself to the bowl of salted peanuts on their table. Mario drank four glasses of wine, and with each glass he became more serious, less talkative. Although he smiled a lot and half-listened to Mike, something seemed to restrain his earlier spontaneity. Mike began to get restless. When it was decided that Mike would sleep at Mario's place, they left the café. Mario hailed a taxi.

Mario lived in a small one-bedroom apartment in the SoHo district. By the time they got there, Mike was half asleep. He nodded out almost instantly on the sofa bed Mario made up for him. Mario picked up a sketchbook and pen, and began drawing a fair likeness of Mike's face. But after several minutes he stopped, switched off the light, and retired to his bedroom. He masturbated before turning in.

Sometime during the night Mike was suddenly wakened by Mario's voice. He was startled to see Mario sitting on the edge of the sofa bed, facing him.

"You were having bad dream," said Mario, putting his hand on Mike's leg.

"Huh? Was I?" Mike yawned.

Mario smoothed Mike's hair with his hand; then he slowly pulled back the bedsheet. Mike lay there, with half-shut eyes, too sleepy to resist Mario's hand fondling his genitals. Then he felt Mario's hot mouth on his stiff penis. Within seconds Mike ejaculated. Like a shadow, Mario slipped out of the room. Mike wiped himself with the sheet, and drifted back to sleep.

In the morning neither of them referred to the incident. Mario was dressed for work, waiting for Mike to finish his coffee and cigarette. "If you like to sleep here tonight," Mario said, "you can phone at my work number. To let me know." He handed Mike a business card.

"Thanks." Mike glanced at the card and slipped it into his pocket.

"You are nice person. I like you," said Mario. "Do you have money?"

"Not much."

He gave Mike a $10 bill. "It is for you."

Outside, Mike wondered where he was. The street looked grimy. The air smelled of exhaust fumes and garbage. He lit a cigarette and started walking uptown. A sign in a bus shelter caught his eye. The silhouette of a sinister-looking man, with white slits for eyes, lurking. He paused to read the bold print. "Every year 500,000 purses and wallets and 100,000 cars are reported stolen in NYC. If you can't afford your own bodyguard, use common sense. It's your best protection." Over NYC Transit Authority and the Big Apple logo someone had scrawled: *Batman was here*.

The sun filtered down through smog. Multiwindowed buildings glared amidst the din of car horns, sirens, jack-hammers. The scurry of people was incessant, insectlike. To escape the heat, and to efface the memory of last night – (a wet dream would have been better, Mike thought), he decided to take in a movie.

Bare-breasted African girls on a movie poster enticed Mike to purchase a ticket to see *Mondo Cane*. It was billed as *Shocking! Sex-citing!* A documentary on bizarre ethnic rituals and sex practices around the world. He bought a 7-Up and a hotdog in the lobby. *Mondo Cane* not only filled him with disgust but angered him. Its lurid cynicism exacerbated his own growing disbelief in commonly accepted human values. Scenes of cannibalism, pig-killing, gluttony, and other vileness reminded him of something his father once said about the human race: it was the equivalent of a highly noxious bacillus parasitizing, and thus slowly despoiling the natural world. He stamped out of the movie house in a murderous mood, loathing the outdoor café crowds, the fashion freaks, the smug cops, the joggers, the dog-walkers, and anyone who looked phony but well-fixed. In his agitation he saw New Yorkers as animals inhabiting a squalid zoo in a concrete jungle. They even spoke a crude, staccato, duck-sounding dialect. *If I had a machine gun . . .*

Mike was drawn again to the world of Times Square. He killed some time in a sex shop. Surrounded by plastic dildoes, phallic candles, domino masks, whips, handcuffs, motorcycle caps, leather codpieces, inflatable life-size love dolls, he leafed through magazines that featured porno-graphic depictions of bondage, fetishism, fellatio, cunnilingus, daisy chains. One customer, a Peter Lorre look-alike, his face flushed and sweaty, kept coughing into a black handkerchief. Mike was tempted to slip a girly mag into his duffel bag, but he didn't want to risk getting caught.

Outside, on 42nd Street, Mike was jostled by the surging crowds. He walked aimlessly, wondering if he should phone Mario. He ogled the half-naked hookers (black ones, white ones) standing on corners, slouched in doorways. He didn't have enough money to buy a kiss.

In the gray dusk Mike strolled past the Astor Hotel. The male hustlers were there, posturing in tight jeans, some with conspicuously bulging crotches. The Meat Rack.

Mike approached a baby-faced, T-shirted hustler and handed him Mario's business card. "This guy's a real score," he said. "Give him a call. He'll make it worth your while." Before the hustler could respond, Mike walked away.

A gang of black teenagers was jiving, finger-popping in front of a brightly lit music store. As Mike drew near, a girl started singing in a rich throaty voice:

They say the neon lights are bright on Broadway;
They say there's always magic in the air . . .

Waiting at a red light, Mike placed his hand on his hip and accidentally elbowed a man beside him. Mike apologized. The man smiled. The light changed. Cars and pedestrians jockeyed for space.

"You must be from out of town," the man said to Mike, keeping abreast of him as they crossed the street.

Surprised, Mike asked: "What makes you say that?"

"You apologized. Courtesy's uncommon here," said the man. "Can I buy you a beer?"

Mike shrugged. "Sure. Why not?" Mike knew he was being cruised, but he felt too tired and hungry to care.

They went to a Broadway bar. The man introduced himself as Lyle. He was of medium height, skinny, in his mid thirties but looked older because of his thinning hair and horn-rimmed glasses, which gave him an owlish look. His clothes and manner suggested a fussy exactitude. Mike soon realized they had little in common other than Lyle's passing interest in him. He told Lyle he was from Detroit, and that he was looking for work. Lyle seemed content to let him do most of the talking. When the waiter served them, Lyle quickly inspected his glass before pouring his Budweiser into it.

"What kind of work do you do?" Mike asked.

"I'm a lighting designer," said Lyle.

Mike looked puzzled. "Lighting designer?"

"In the theatre. I design the lighting for plays, ballets, operas . . . "

"Oh, like Broadway shows."

"Sometimes," said Lyle. "I'm afraid the Great White Way is rather gray now."

"What do you mean?" asked Mike. He was beginning to feel like a hick.

"It's off-season." Lyle half-smiled in a way that Mike found patronizing. "Instead of sitting here," said Lyle, "why don't we go to my place. Bars give me a headache. I'm not myself in them. If that's okay with you."

Mike lit a cigarette. He didn't want to appear too eager or vulnerable.

"Unless you have other plans," Lyle said.

Mike shifted nervously in his chair, an animal at bay. He didn't have enough money for a room at the Y. He wasn't keen about spending the night with Lyle, whom he found odd yet harmless, and unappealing, too. He was reluctant to phone his father collect and ask him for money. He was tired of roaming the streets. "Soon as I finish my beer," he said.

"Take your time. I don't live far."

The apartment Mike entered was roomy, high-ceilinged, and elegantly furnished. He stood there, trying to take it all in: the Oriental rug, potted plants, goldfish aquarium, bookcases crammed with books, black leather reclining chair, batik wall hangings, playbills, photographs, painted Moroccan coffee table, track lighting . . .

"You have a marvelous place," Mike said.

"Thank-you. It's my refuge – when the world is too much with me. Sit down. Relax. Beer, whiskey, or wine?"

"I'll have some wine."

"Red or white?"

"Red. If it's no trouble, do you have any cheese and crackers, or whatever?"

"No trouble at all," said Lyle. "I'll see what I can do."

While Lyle was out of the room, Mike got up to look at the pictures on the walls. He was amazed to see the late James Dean and a younger-looking Lyle in a black-and-white group photograph. Handwritten with a ball-point on a playbill of *Suddenly Last Summer* were the words: *For Lyle – Tennessee Williams*. Next he read the inscription on a plaque: *Lyle Watson. Village Voice Off-Broadway Obie Award – 1960 – for Best Lighting Design.*

Presently Lyle returned with a platter of finger food and two short-stemmed glasses of red wine. Mike turned around. "I didn't know you were famous," he said.

"An overstatement," Lyle replied, setting the platter on the coffee table.

"How well did you know James Dean?" Mike asked,

"I met him only once."

"What was he like?"

Lyle shrugged. "Moody." He gestured toward the food. "Help yourself."

"Thanks." Mike took a slice of carrot and a crustless egg-salad sandwich from the platter. "I used to belong to the James Dean fan club. I guess you've met a lot of movie stars."

"A few." Lyle lit an Old Gold cigarette.

"Which ones?"

Lyle took a sip of wine. "Well . . . Shelley Winters. She's a big crybaby, as I recall. And Monty Clift. Who can forget Montgomery Clift? A dear actor-friend of mine was madly in love with him."

Surprised, Mike let Lyle's remark pass. He reached for another sandwich. Lyle got up and put a record on the stereo. It was Dvorak's "New World" Symphony.

"How did you become a lighting designer?" Mike asked out of politeness. "It sounds like a complicated job."

"Well, let's see." Lyle gazed up at the ceiling. "A lighting designer needs to know just about everything there is to know about light. What is light? How is it produced, modified, controlled? Do you know what I mean?"

"Kind of – "

"Light is the ultimate tool of designers. Their whole career is devoted to evoking human responses from the use of light on stage, in TV and films. *Fiat lux*. Let there be light," Lyle said in a high voice, flinging up his arms histrionically. "Yes, I suppose it is rather complicated and technical. But we're not here to talk shop. I love swimming, ballet, classical music. Do you like classical music?"

"Rock 'n' roll," said Mike.

"I suppose it has its place," Lyle said, and glanced at his wristwatch. "I have a frantic day tomorrow. Perhaps you'd like to shower – before we turn in."

Mike flinched. Although he was tired, the thought of sleeping in the same bed with Lyle repelled him. He was certain, too, that Lyle expected sexual favors. He also noticed that his cigarette pack was empty. *What am I doing here?* he thought. He tried to stall for time.

"I once saw a play in Detroit called *The Connection*. About dope addicts. Would that play be regarded as Off-Broadway?"

"Awfully Off-Broadway," Lyle sniffed.

"I think the wine gave me a headache," said Mike.

"We'll take care of that." Lyle got up and left the room. Mike felt nervous, done in. He considered leaving.

"I'm in the kitchen," Lyle called out. "Come hither."

Lyle handed Mike two white pills. Mike eyed them doubtfully. "What are they?"

"Common aspirin. Guaranteed to make your headache go away."

Mike swallowed them with a glass of tap water.

"Now why don't you take a good hot shower," said Lyle. "You'll feel better."

When Mike emerged from the bathroom after his shower, he felt refreshed but curiously light-headed. Lyle was sitting in a chair, with his glasses off, legs crossed, smoking a cigarette. He had put on a maroon-colored lounging robe. The sight of him, with his small head and long slender, hairy limbs reminded Mike of a spider monkey he'd once seen at the zoo. Mike had only his jeans on.

"You have a nice lean body. Clear skin," Lyle said, leering at him. "You look fresh and clean."

Lyle's compliment made Mike recall the meat-inspector at the Y. "Where do you want me to sleep?" he asked uncertainly.

Lyle peered at him. His tongue darted over his thin lips. "With me, of course. I know you're not some pickup; but I have only one bed."

Mike avoided watching Lyle disrobe. As they lay together in bed, with the table lamp on, Mike's tension mounted. Lyle reached over and put his hand on Mike's thigh. Mike moved uneasily.

"Why don't you take off your shorts?" Lyle said. "I want to hold your cock."

"Not yet," Mike gritted.

"What's the matter?"

"Have you got a cigarette?" With an effort of will, Mike tried to steady himself. "Those pills you gave me . . . Were they aspirin?"

"Yes. Why?"

"I feel funny." Mike took a deep drag on the cigarette. He could sense Lyle playing with himself under the bedsheet.

"You're nervous," Lyle said, and began caressing Mike's thigh, tugging at the elastic band on his shorts. "Try to relax. I want to feel your cock getting big and hard."

As if in slow motion, Mike carefully butted his cigarette in the ashtray beside the bed. Then his mind went blank with rage. He smashed his fist in Lyle's face, and then he struck him twice more. Lyle cried out from the shock of the blows, cringing under them. Blood spurted from his mouth and nose. Clutching a pillow, he tried to roll on his side to protect himself. The bedsheet was spattered with blood. Mike yanked him out of bed and began beating him. A tripod and camera crashed to the floor. He wrenched Lyle's arm, and heard something crack. "DON'T KILL ME!" Lyle cried out in pain and terror. Mike grabbed him by the neck and shoulder, like a battering ram, and dashed him headfirst against the wall. Lyle sank to the floor, his naked body smeared with blood. There was blood everywhere; the parquet floor was slippery with it. "I can't move . . . Please don't kill me," Lyle pleaded.

"I'm not gonna kill you," Mike muttered, panting, his rage spent. "Where's your money?" He quickly got into his clothes.

"I'll write you a check. For any amount."

"I NEED CASH! WHERE IS IT?"

Lyle coughed. "In – in the laundry hamper." He coughed again. "Oh . . . my ribs," he whimpered.

Mike tore open the lid of the hamper, scattering clothes every which way. At the bottom of the hamper was a roll of $20 bills held together with a rubber band. Mike thrust the roll into his pocket. He turned toward Lyle. Lyle was unconscious.

Outside, Mike felt weightless, giddy, high on adrenalin. He ran down the shadowy street, murmuring *mouth, ass, cock, cunt* over and over in a kind of jerky cadence. He turned a corner. And then another corner. Each time he heard a siren he froze. Each time he saw a police car he ducked in among the shadows of buildings. His shirt was soaked with clammy sweat. His hands felt sticky. He looked at his hands under a streetlamp. They were covered with blood.

On a side street, Mike glanced inside an auto-repair shop. A mechanic was working under the hood of a car. Save for the mechanic the shop looked deserted. Mike slipped into the rest room. He washed the blood off his hands.

Bypassing Times Square, Mike walked until he came to the Port Authority Bus Terminal. He went inside and headed directly for the men's room. A tall, gaunt black man in shabby clothes said to him: "Whattaya on, man?" Ignoring him, Mike bent over a washbasin and began splashing cold water on his face. He dried his face with a paper towel, and then he looked at himself in the mirror. His face was ashen, his eyes bloodshot. On the wall, beside the mirror, he saw some graffiti. It read: *Help the police. Beat up yourself.* When he felt sufficiently calm, he went to the ticket counter and bought a one-way bus ticket to Detroit.

One cloudy morning in mid-November Mike Simmons boarded the tunnel bus to Detroit. After going through U.S. Customs and Immigration, he walked to a nearby restaurant, went inside, and sat there for almost an hour drinking coffee and smoking cigarettes. When he left the restaurant, he walked over to a telephone booth and dialed the operator. Then he deposited several coins in the slot. The phone rang four times before a man's voice answered.

"Hello."

"Lyle Watson, please."

"This is he," the voice said. "Who's calling?"

Mike Simmons hung up the receiver.

A LODGING FOR THE NIGHT

It took us almost two hours to drive from Wolfville to Halifax. Gray sheets of rain with grayer patches of fog all the way. I could barely see beyond the hood of our rental car. The metronomic monotony of the windshield wipers had rubbed my nerves raw. While I smoked, Frances dozed beside me. For the past four days we'd been in Wolfville. Socializing, sight-seeing, mostly preparing for the opening of Frances's exhibition of black-and-white photographs at the Acadia Art Gallery. Her show was a success, attended by many. It was my first visit to Nova Scotia. I felt some connection with the province. It was my mother's birthplace: New Waterford, to be exact.

We reached Halifax about noon. It was still raining, but not as heavily. In the rain, the city looked old and bleak. I was eager to explore the downtown streets, soak up the atmosphere of the waterfront. According to a travel brochure, Halifax has the oldest naval dockyard in North America.

We stopped for coffee and poppy-seed bagels at a restaurant on Spring Garden Road. I told Frances I'd read somewhere that the word Halifax meant "holy hair" or "sea hair." Frances was fidgeting with some papers in her handbag. "You mean, like seaweed?" she said.

I had always wanted to visit Halifax. In my mind the city evoked ghostly images of World War II. Soldiers, sailors, warships, troopships. I also associated Halifax with a Canadian poet I'd once read about: Bertram Warr. It was

in Halifax, on Christmas Eve 1938, that Warr stowed away
on a passenger liner bound for England. The poet was
only 25 when he was killed in action aboard an RAF
Halifax bomber, over Germany.

Frances wanted to visit art galleries. (She'd been to
Halifax twice before.) I wanted to see the *Bluenose 2* racing schooner, the Maritime Museum of the Atlantic, and
historic Pier 21. We flipped a coin. Frances lost.

"We don't have time to traipse around like tourists,"
she said, and reminded me that we had to find a lodging
for the night. We were flying home to Toronto the next
day, and the airport was 25 miles from downtown. I gave
in, after she promised me a seafood dinner of my choice.
Food was her way of appeasing me. For a visual artist, she
was bossy and practical. Whenever we traveled together,
I was content to let her take care of routes, schedules,
reservations. We had been lovers for six years, and knew
each other's habits well. We were both middle-aged, though
I was eleven years older. She often teased me about it.

Frances phoned around for our overnight accommodations. Unlike her, I wasn't fond of bed-and-breakfast
establishments. They might be homey and all; but a B and
B always made me feel like an intruder. Smoking was usually forbidden, and you couldn't fart or belch lest someone might hear you. I preferred the casual privacy of a
motel. I couldn't be choosy though. Frances was footing
the cost.

Mist, rain and fog were rolling in from the ocean when
Frances returned to the car. "I found us a place," she said
with satisfaction. "A guesthouse."

We spent most of the afternoon—or, rather, Frances
did, visiting art galleries. I waited in the car, reading a
paperback—David Morrell's *Black Evening*. At one point,
seeing how glum and restless I looked, Frances suggested

we go to a secondhand bookstore that had caught her eye because of the tabby cat in the window. She was delighted to find a paperback copy of Ansel Adams' *The Negative*.

A parking ticket was stuck under the wiper of our car. The ticket was wet but legible. "Fifteen dollars!" I snorted in disgust. "For a goddamn meter violation!" I banged the meter with my fist. "It's highway robbery!" I was about to tear up the ticket. Frances snatched it from me.

"I think a nice quiet dinner will make us both feel better," she said.

"Good idea. I know it's April, but all this rain is beginning to soften my brain."

"It's whetting my appetite," she punned.

I poked her playfully in the ribs. "Do you think the rain'll hurt the rhubarb?"

"Not if it's in cans," she replied.

"What if it rains can openers?"

She couldn't remember the punch line.

"Then it'll be open season on rhubarb."

"Ha-ha. Very funny."

"No wonder Scotia means *darkness*," I said.

"What?"

"Scotia. It means *darkness* in Greek. The etymology. Nova – Latin for new. Nova Scotia. *New darkness*."

We had an excellent lobster dinner at McKelvie's, near the harbor. Frances had a carafe of white wine. I had rum and Coke.

"We'll unpack our things at the guesthouse, and then relax," she said. "I'm so tired."

Outside, it was drizzly dark. I drove around Citadel Hill, and almost ran a red light. Poring over a city map, Frances barked directions at me. "On Robie Street. Then turn right. Granny's Guesthouse. It's across from the North Common."

"Granny's Guesthouse?" I said uncertainly. "Sounds like a bad fairy tale."

"There it is!" she said, pointing out the house.

"I suppose we're Hansel and Gretel," I muttered.

Granny's Guesthouse looked shabby-genteel. It was an old, two-storey frame house with clapboard siding painted pale blue with white trim. It had a small front porch. Had it not been for the feeble glow of the porch-light, the house would have looked deserted. There was no driveway, so I parked the car on the street. We unloaded most of our luggage, including Frances's expensive camera equipment. While I was locking the car, she went into the house to see Granny.

As soon as I stepped inside, I was disappointed.

Although the hallway was tidy, the carpet was threadbare and the lighting dim. On the walls were several framed black-and-white photos of unsmiling men and women. A few of the men were in their military uniforms. Midway down the hall, beside a closed door, stood a grandfather clock. The house was strangely silent.

"It smells musty," I said, making a face.

"It was only thirty-five dollars for two," Frances huffed.

"Look, there's Granny," I said. "Embalmed."

Sitting in a wooden rocking chair was a large doll about four feet in length. Whoever made the doll had designed it to resemble the archetypal grandmother. The doll looked weirdly lifelike. Although wrinkleless, its face was pinched and pointy-chinned, the prim little mouth fixed in a mocking smile. The blue eyes, glass or plastic, peered out from behind granny glasses. On the doll's head was a faded white bonnet. A pale blue Mother Hubbard was wrapped loosely about the doll, and partly covering the dress was a white pinafore. The doll's feet were slippered.

"It looks creepy," I said, and gave the rocker a nudge with my foot.

Frances marveled at the craftwork. "I think it's cute. Quaint but cute."

Suddenly the door beside the grandfather clock squeaked open, then closed softly.

"Welcome to the Bates Motel," I joked.

"Shhh! Keep your voice down," Frances whispered.

"Why are you whispering?"

She frowned at me.

"Yeah, I might wake the dead. I bet we're the only guests in this funeral parlor."

Our room was on the main floor, at the rear of the guesthouse. It was a bedroom-sized room, with hideous flowered wallpaper. I couldn't see the room for the furniture. There was enough stuff in it to furnish two rooms its size. A double bed, two armchairs, a straight-backed chair, a chest of drawers, a night table and lamp, a card table, and a portable TV. The room was cluttered with tacky bric-a-brac, doilies galore in garish colors.

"Can you smell something in here?" I wrinkled up my face.

"Yes. It smells like faulty plumbing," Frances said, unpacking her toiletries.

"Or something dead. Probably a rat rotting away under the floorboards."

"Oh, stop complaining. What I need is a long hot shower," she said, and left the room.

I took off my jacket and shoes. I opened the window a few inches, then I switched on the TV. Nothing caught my interest, so I shut it off. I lit a cigarette despite the *Thankyou For Not Smoking* sign on the wall. I heard Frances talking to someone out in the hallway. I opened the door and looked out. I was astonished to see an elderly woman – dressed exactly like the doll.

When Frances returned, I was pacing the room, smoking a cigarette. She poured some Scotch into a plastic cup.

"This room makes me claustrophobic," I grumbled.

"The bed's not very comfortable," she said. Her head, wrapped in a white towel, was propped on a pillow.

I lay down on the bed. "You're right. It's a torture-rack. We'll both have backaches by morning." I got up and sprawled in one of the armchairs.

"Aren't you tired?" she asked.

"On edge."

"This might help." She held out the plastic cup.

"You know I don't like Scotch. I keep thinking of that doll in the rocking chair."

"Whistler's mother. What about it?"

"It's grotesque, morbid. It reminds me of a corpse."

"Maybe the owner keeps it there to discourage burglars."

"I saw the owner – Granny, or whatever her name is. She was dressed just like the doll!"

"So what? I think you're overreacting."

Somehow the doll and my glimpse of Granny reminded me of a domestic tragedy my mother had related to me long ago. "Did I ever tell you about my Uncle Leo?" I said.

"Is this a bedtime story?" She sipped at her Scotch.

"He was my mother's eldest brother. A quiet sort of man; had the biggest hands I've ever seen. Anyway, his second wife went mad. She must have been in her mid sixties at the time. One night she dumped a bushel of dead leaves on him as he lay asleep in bed. After that, things got worse. Sometimes she'd sit in the basement all day, talking to herself. Then her cooking became erratic. My uncle found sliced earthworms in his *radicchio* salad. She'd run around naked inside the house, cursing and screaming. She even dug a hole in their backyard; said her baby had died and she wanted to bury it. My uncle didn't know what to do. He was afraid she'd kill herself, or poison his food." I paused to stub out my cigarette. "Finally, he had her committed to a mental hospital. She died there."

"Holy crow!" Frances said sadly. "I guess old people, especially if they're lonely and they feel unwanted, sometimes do strange things just to remind themselves they're alive."

"She didn't go mad because of loneliness," I said. "My uncle was a kind man."

"I didn't mean it that way," she said, then she smiled. "I wonder what you'll be like when you're an old man."

"A sensitive ogre."

"That'll be an improvement." She puckered up her lips. "But I love you."

I undressed, climbed into bed, and snuggled close to her.

Sometime during the night I wakened with a cramp in my neck. Frances stirred in her sleep. I listened to the sound of her breathing. The rain had stopped, but the room felt cool and damp. When I got out of bed to close the window, I thought I heard a soft rustle outside our door. I strained my ears to listen. Silence. I put on my robe and stood by the door for a moment. Then I opened the door slowly and stepped into the hallway. Suddenly the clock chimed, startling me. Off the hallway to the right was the bathroom. I stole past it, unable to resist looking at the doll, as if it were beckoning me. It sat there, the dim light glinting off its spectacles, the eyes watching me, the tight little mouth mocking my presence. I gazed at it with loathing. I shuddered.

When I opened the door to our room, Frances woke up.

"What's the matter?" she mumbled sleepily.

"Nothing. I was in the bathroom."

Unable to sleep, I sat in an armchair – thinking – impatient for daylight – listening to the house sleep.

I dozed off.

When next I woke, the clock radio showed almost four a.m. Again I heard a noise. This time it was a distinct scuffling sound outside the door. I sat transfixed, wondering if it was a rat. The sound ceased, then continued. Along the narrow lighted space at the bottom of the door I saw a faint shadow moving. I tiptoed over to the bed and nudged Frances gently.

"Huh? What are you doing?"

"There's someone outside our door," I whispered.

"Is the door locked?"

"Yes . . . Listen."

She sat up. "I don't hear anything."

"It's the second time tonight I've heard noises."

"Well, go and see – " she grumbled. "Please . . . Let me sleep."

I wondered if I was trying to frighten Frances into believing me. *Maybe it is my nerves*, I thought. An auditory hallucination. I sprang towards the door and flung it open. No one – nothing – was there. As I was about to close the door, I heard a slow throbbing. It sounded slightly rhythmic. I couldn't identify the sound. Curious, I crept along the hallway. Then I stopped abruptly. *The rocking chair was rocking.* "What the hell!" I exclaimed aloud. Baffled, I stared at the doll, as if hypnotized, until the rocking chair came to a stop.

When I dashed into the room, the light was on. Frances was awake, a glass of water in her hand. She looked angry.

"Why are you so restless?" she said. "If you can't sleep, go out for a walk."

"The rocking chair was moving. I saw it," I said.

"It's just your imagination."

"I saw it moving."

"Probably a draft or something."

"A draft? I doubt it. I'm not talking about ghosts and haunted houses; but this damn place hasn't felt right since we got here."

"Are you blaming me?"

"No, I'm not blaming you. But something's going on. I feel like knocking on Granny's door – "

"Don't you dare – "

"Why not?"

"Because I'm tired. I want to sleep," she said irritably. "You keep waking me up."

"The rocking chair *was* moving. I saw it moving."

"Please go to sleep," she said, and switched off the table lamp.

I opened my eyes and blinked. It was a few minutes after seven o'clock. Frances was already up, packing our suitcases and, it seemed to me, making a lot of unnecessary noise. I stretched my arms and yawned. "What a hellish night."

"Yes. Thanks to you." She gave me a sullen look. "C'mon – time to get up."

"Somebody's in a foul mood," I said.

"I'm tired. That bed was like sleeping on bricks. My left shoulder is sore . . . And you were acting like a lunatic."

"I kept hearing noises all night. And that ugly doll – "

"I'm sure there's some explanation."

"Yeah, a poltergeist," I said sarcastically.

I climbed out of bed, gave her a quick kiss, and went over to the window. The morning sky was overcast. The window looked out on a backyard that had a stunted willow tree, a weedy lawn, a few small rosebushes, a weath-

ered picnic table, and a green Adirondack chair. Some of
the chair's slats were missing. The view depressed me.

In less than twenty minutes we were ready to leave.

"You go on ahead," said Frances, scanning the room.
"I don't want to forget anything."

In the hallway I almost stepped on a dark gray object
that looked like a dead mouse. I was overcome by revul-
sion. As I approached the doll, I resisted an impulse to
push it off the rocking chair. I banged a suitcase against
the rocker instead. And then I hurried out the door.

Satisfied that she hadn't overlooked any of her belongings, Frances was on her way out when a door opened,
and Granny appeared, holding the door ajar. Granny was
in her late sixties; short, stout, bespectacled, and slightly
hunchbacked.

"Leaving so early?" said Granny. "I've just made a pot
of tea. Would you care for a cup?"

"Thank-you, but we have a plane to catch," said
Frances.

Just then a big black cat sauntered out the door, and
meowed.

"What a beautiful cat," Frances said, bending down to
stroke its glossy fur.

"That's Charlie," Granny said fondly. "He's supposed
to be the watch-cat; but he prefers playing and having a
good time. Don't you, Charlie? I don't let him go outside.
Too many cars. I usually let Charlie have the run of the
house, late at night, when my guests are asleep."

The cat began rubbing up against Frances's leg.

"I hope you enjoyed your room and had a good night's
rest," said Granny. "Young people travel so much nowa-
days."

"Yes, the room was nice and cozy," said Frances. "Oh,
by the way – that doll of yours looks so real. It gave my
friend quite a start."

"Oh my, yes, the doll. My dear sister made it. She passed away last year. God rest her soul. She won many prizes for her dolls. Charlie was her cat."

Suddenly the cat jumped up onto the rocking chair.

"Tut-tut!" exclaimed Granny. "Sometimes Charlie's manners are atrocious." She went to fetch the cat. It meowed.

Outside, a light rain was falling. I waited in the car and smoked a cigarette. I honked the horn twice.

"What took you so long?" I grumped when Frances got into the car.

"I was talking to Granny." Frances fastened her seat belt.

"Did you tell her about last night?"

"Of course not."

"I wish the hell I had." I started the car.

"Oh, stop it. She's just a little old lady eking out a living."

"There was a dead mouse in the hallway," I said.

"Yeah, a dead toy mouse. I saw it."

I grunted, and drove off.

"And guess what – " said Frances, half-smiling. "Granny has a big black cat."

THE VALENTINE

When I was in grade 5, the prettiest girl in my class gave me the biggest and reddest valentine card, with the inscription: *E.F. loves L.G.* Was I thrilled? Yes. Did I blush? I think my blood must have shone through my face. I remember she had green eyes, blonde hair, was tall for her age, and I once got the strap for pelting her with snowballs at recess. Then my memory fades. Her family moved to California. I never saw her again.

In my dream, *it was a snowy night and I was walking through the streets of my hometown. I saw her standing alone outside a movie theatre whose brightly lighted marquee was blank. We recognized each other immediately. She had blossomed into a beautiful young woman. We embraced. O bliss! Suddenly we were in a luxurious bedroom. Pink walls and ceiling. A four-poster bed. A white dressing table. Red and white roses in a crystal vase. We drank wine . . . we kissed . . . we drank more wine . . . she confessed that she was a virgin . . . our kissing became more intense . . .*

At this moment someone strikes a match . . . coughs, and that wakes me up. I awaken weary, dry-mouthed, and hung over.

"You were talkin' in your sleep," a woman says, exhaling cigarette smoke. The woman has bleached blonde hair. Her mascara is smudged. The room I'm in is dingy, the air stagnant, musty. The woman spills out of bed and pads listlessly to the window. "It's snowin'," she yawns. Framed in the window-light of morning she looks dull, sluttish.

Her buttocks and thighs are lumpy with fat. I realize she is someone I picked up in a bar last night. She turns bedward. As I reach for my wristwatch, I notice a blood-stain on the bedsheet. "My period came," she says, pretending to pout.

The stain was heartshaped.

AN ARABIAN DAY'S ENTERTAINMENT

Morning overtook Scheherazade, and she lapsed into silence.

In a private, palm-shaded courtyard in the desert a tourist, traveling alone, is sipping mint tea and smoking kif. The day is hot, the air dry, brilliant, with a sun that burns a white hole in the sky. This morning, during breakfast, the tourist's overnight companion – a young Arab woman with kohl-farded eyes – taught him the four recognized stages in the ripening of a date: *kimri, khalal, rutab, tamar.* The tourist softly incants the Arabic words, as if to cast a spell on himself by recalling what the young woman said. *The date is green in the kimri stage. Khalal is when the date reaches its full size and turns reddish yellow. Rutab is when the date loses its bright coloring, and begins to ripen and soften. When the date has dried out and is fully matured, it is tamar – cured – and will keep for a long time without spoiling. The date needs six months to ripen. It is the bread of the desert* . . . and an aphrodisiac, he remembers. The male date flowers are eaten as a salad with lemon juice.

The tourist takes a *deglet noor* – "daughter of light" – a delicious, semidry date from a dish the woman has graciously placed beside him. He pops the date into his mouth, bites it, and spits out the hard pit. He chews the date slowly, running his tongue across the texture of the meat, savoring its sweetness, tasting the woman's deep kisses in the ripe flesh of this ancient fruit, this *bread of the desert* fed with sunlight, praised by the prophet

Muhammad, and growing to the sound of the wind scrap-
ing the palm fronds one against the other.

In the desert, time is measured by the ripening of a date.

SIGN LANGUAGE

Elliott dashed inside the subway car just before the doors closed. He sat down, looked at his digital wristwatch. *12:11 a.m.* He hopes his wife isn't waiting up for him. The thought of having to explain his lateness makes him tense. His eyes rove over the passengers in the car: a woman with a small white poodle; a young Chinese couple; a teenager with green hair, nose ring, skateboard; a bald-headed man doing a crossword puzzle. Elliott closes his eyes for a moment, feels the rumble of the subway train as it growls along the track. He thinks of the woman he made love with only an hour ago, in her apartment. He and the woman – a childless divorcee – teach ESL at the same night school. A twinge of guilt makes him grimace. He tries to blank out the woman's image with the lie he will tell his wife, the crafty excuse to allay suspicion. He hates lying to her about his infidelities. She seems to have a sixth sense of his lies. He knows she no longer trusts him; yet he always denies her accusations. What was it the Roman poet Ovid said? *If your wife catches you in bed with another woman, deny it.* Or words to that effect. Elliott knows the truth can be more harmful than a lie. The night he came home drunk and his wife noticed his ring finger was bare. He had removed his wedding band at a singles bar and then forgotten about it. He made up a credible story involving the police. She believed him that time. His wife's suspicions are aroused by smells, stains, moods, even his behavior in bed. Although he loves his wife and is certain of her faithfulness, he is prone to cynicism, and sometimes wonders if deceit and mistrust are the essence of human relationships. While he is brooding on his situation, a man and a woman board the car together. They look middle-aged. A handsome couple. They sit down across the aisle from Elliott, facing toward the front of the car. They begin gesturing to each other with hands, arms, heads. Elliott suddenly realizes they are both deaf. To avoid staring at them, he reads the advertisements in the car. Yet he can see their reflections in the dark blank window. He is aware of their fluttering hands. Their gestures seem spastic. They appear to be communicating intimate and important things to each other. At one point the deaf woman glances at Elliott in a friendly manner but he looks away, embarrassed. The train's sounds jar Elliott's nerves. He stares at his own hands. *Can a deaf person lie in sign language?* he wonders. He steals glances at the couple, tries to read something in their faces. Are they naming abstract concepts and reasoning? Metaphors? He doesn't know. He thinks of his adult students learning English as a second language. "Each new word you learn is a new thought," he always impresses on them. The train clatters into a nearly deserted station stop. Elliott grabs hold of his black leather briefcase and steps out of the car and onto the platform.

Outside, it was snowing. As Elliott hurried along the street, he thought of the deaf couple. "I won't say a word to her," he said to himself. "Not one word." And he shook his head from side to side, as though to bolster his resolve.

BACKGROUND MUSIC

Under a shady tree a young man lies sleeping. Around him the wooded landscape is bathed in the golden light of a southern California summer afternoon. The man is clad in black mesh briefs. His muscular body is extremely hairy, but more noticeable are his pointed ears, his goatee, and the two small horns on his head. Suddenly two young women – a brunette and a redhead – appear. They are barefoot and diaphanously veiled. Each wears a chaplet of leaves. They see the sleeping man, and slowly approach him. The redhead whispers something in the brunette's ear. They laugh lightly, and begin to caress the man. He wakens, opens his eyes, and sits up. The women scamper away, their luminous forms shimmering through the leafy shadows. He rubs his eyes, and says: "I would immortalize those nymphs: their flesh-pink coloring so airy light, it floats like gossamer. Was it a dream I loved?" He picks up his panpipe lying beside a bowl of purple grapes, and plays. While he is playing, the two women return. They seem coy yet curious.

"May I play your flute? " *says the redhead.*

"May I have some grapes?" *says the brunette.*

Soon the two women are taking turns fellating him and sitting astride his face. At the height of the man's passion they suddenly stop, and dash off into the shadowy woods. He springs to his feet and gives chase. But the women have vanished. Finding himself alone, he says: "Who cares? Their hair is tangled on my horns. Others will draw me on to-

ward happiness. My passion is like a pomegranate; and my blood, kindled by some chance fire, flows for the eternal swarming of desire." He retrieves his panpipe, plays a few notes, and then tosses it aside. "My body and soul succumb, " he says, "to the hot silence of the sun. Now I must sleep to forget. Farewell, sweet nymphs. I shall see the shadows you have become." He stretches himself on the grass and closes his eyes.

"Okay, CUT!" the director barked. "Let's wrap it. *Très* sexy, Kelly." He patted the redhead Kelly Carnal on her shamrock-tattooed buttock. Kelly had the makings of a porn star. She had recently appeared in a film with Marilyn Chambers.

Nearby, two cameramen began disassembling their equipment. The lighting technician lit a cigarette and chatted with the makeup artist – a fortyish, platinum-blonde ex-fluffer with silicone-enlarged breasts. The makeup artist was the director's fourth and current wife. The director was her third husband. According to porn industry gossip, she was having a clandestine affair with a black deejay just to spite her husband, whom she suspected of philandering with Kelly.

"Well, it's not Daphnis and Chloe," said the director, "but we got some nice shots, great close-ups." He removed his mirror sunglasses. He was a short, swarthy, hypertense man in his fifties. "The one thing that still bothers me," he said, "is the synchronism of the background music with the action." He turned to face the actor Jeff Steele who was drinking a can of iced tea. "Jeff, in case you've forgotten, we're not doing a bunch of loops. We're shooting a ninety-minute feature. You sounded unconvincing. There was no expression in your voice."

"It's not me, Harvey, it's the corny dialogue," Jeff grumbled. "*My passion is like a pomegranate.* Nobody talks like that. The character sounds like a dork."

"And that little chase you gave – " said the director. "I've seen guys on crutches move faster. I wanted something intense, fluid, urgent – "

"Track and field ain't my thing," Jeff said resentfully. "And I'm all out of body fluids."

One of the cameramen laughed.

"Pity," said the director. "You're supposed to be a satyr. Act like one. You were blah. No emotion, no style. We'll have to do a goddamn compilation." He looked around at the others.

"Can we get out of this bush, Harvey?" Kelly said fretfully. "It's hot, and I'm getting eaten alive by mosquitoes."

"Ah, you poor thing!" the makeup artist mimicked her. "How will I ever cover those little pink bumps?"

"At least I don't have your bulges," Kelly retorted, tossing her head disdainfully.

The lighting technician cleared his throat.

"ENOUGH!" shouted the director. "Now – all of you – please listen up."

The others stopped what they were doing and looked at the director.

"Debussy's *Afternoon of a Faun* lasts about ten minutes," said the director. "We've been here almost three hours; and time is money. I needn't remind you the producer doesn't like exceeding the budget. This film must be cost-effective. Now I'll say it for the last time. The music opens with the sound of the faun's flute. The arabesque is repeated with shifting harmonies and delicate orchestral color. I wanted more tenderness and foreplay to go with the soft tremolos of strings, the little clusters of woodwind tone – "

"Hell, this ain't Carnegie Hall," Jeff interrupted. "It's only a skin flick." He began dressing quickly.

"BUT I WANT IT TO BE ART!" the director growled.

"What's so arty about some dude balling a couple of nymphos?" asked Jeff.

Kelly gave Jeff a withering look. "Look who's talking. Mister Viagra. Go hump your motorbike, Jeff. I'm the one driving a Porsche."

"Whoopee shit!" said Jeff. "Who parks it for you?"

"Are you through flapping your lips?" the director said to Jeff, and then wagged his finger at him. "Listen, stud. I direct, you get wood. Like Johnny Wadd, you got more cock than brains. A wood nymph is *not* a nympho. In Greek and Roman mythology, a wood nymph or dryad is one of the minor divinities of nature. And the *Afternoon of a Faun* is the most sensual piece of orchestral music ever composed. It's a tone poem that evokes the pagan world. It creates a musical language extremely suggestive and erotic. The listener is unable to distinguish between fantasy and reality. Debussy declared that in composing *Afternoon of a Faun* he followed Mallarmé's poem line by line."

Covering his mouth with his hand, Jeff faked a loud yawn.

"Harvey used to play the violin," said the makeup artist, with mock seriousness.

The director bristled. "Not as well as you played the skin flute," he said acidly.

There was a titter of laughter. Although it was obvious to the director that none of the cast and film crew understood what he was talking about, he enjoyed expounding on the virtues of classical music. Sometimes he regaled them with anecdotes of great composers' sex lives: Franz Liszt was a lecher; Schubert died of syphilis; Tchaikovsky was gay; Chopin lived with a woman who dressed like a man. However, they knew him only as a director and writer of X-rated videos that sold well. His last film, *Musical*

Beds, had been a real blockbuster. *Adult Video News* had praised it to the sky. It was even on the Internet. The director had strong ideals concerning art. As a young man he had hoped to become a concert violinist. He had studied for a time at the Juilliard School of Music. As it turned out, he lacked perseverance and the capacity for unremitting work. He discovered he was more adept at playing on the heartstrings of women than on any stringed instrument. An accidental injury to his hand and an eventual $100 a day coke habit put an end to his career. He drifted into the world of pornography, and found it lucrative. It was his driving personal ambition to render an orgiastic version of Wagner's *Tannhauser* in a feature-length film.

"I'm still not sure which rendition of the *Faun* is more evocative," the director mused. "Herbert von Karajan's Berliner Philharmoniker, or Jean Martinon and the French National Radio Orchestra."

"Flip a coin," Jeff quipped.

The director exploded with wrath. "The next film you're in," he roared at Jeff, "I'll personally see to it that you're gagged. NOW SHUT UP! Do you think I'm here to get a goddamn suntan?" He paused, then continued in a calm voice. "Now everybody listen up. I'm trying to fuse the erotic with the so-called pornographic. And to my mind, the only difference between the two is *aesthetic* – meaning *beautiful*, as distinguished from what's palatable, moral, and useful. People like Jeff are easily bored. My job as a director is to make them feel they're not only viewing sensational sex but having a beautiful intellectual and emotional experience. A double whammy." He smiled. "Now there's soft-core and there's hard-core. I don't sell soft sex. And I don't peddle kiddie porn. Those who peddle that stuff should be hanged and quartered. But I want the hard-core to be artistic. Like the Kama Sutra, like the erotic sculptures on those temples in India. I want my films to attract women too, and to turn them on. I demand good acting and realistic scenarios. A woman squatting to pee is more sexually educational than an ejaculating penis. Art and pornography make strange bedfellows. Unlike the church and the law, pornography doesn't try to socialize the penis . . ." He paused to wipe his brow with a Kleenex. "Anyway. As I was saying. You may think my concern with background music is excessive. But I can assure you it's not. Definitely not. Every detail counts. It's money in the bank. I'm providing a service. We're all of us providing a valuable service – to millions of Americans. To their wish-fulfillment fantasies. In a sense, we're sociobiologists. Keepers of the dream." He stopped suddenly to observe the effect his words had on everyone. There was a moment of fidgety silence.

"Can we go now, Harvey?" Kelly said in a whining voice.

"Yes, let's get out of here before we're all arrested for lewd trespassing," said the makeup artist. "I've seen and heard enough for one day."

"The day's far from over, my dear," the director said, pocketing his pen and notebook. "Oh, and one more thing –" He paused till he had everyone's attention. "Don't forget the orgy scene at the pool tonight. Shooting starts at eight sharp. The producer will be there. We're using his pool. Any problems?"

"Are my horns waterproof?" Jeff wisecracked.

An electrician snorted: "Don't worry, Jeff. Stick a cork in your ass. You'll float."

"Okay, let's break camp," the director barked.

The troupe gathered their gear and ambled away through the woods.

On a dirt road, beside a tree-shaded creek, a black Jaguar XJS, a custom van, a Harley-Davidson motorcycle, and a shamrock-green Porsche convertible were parked one behind the other.

THE WHITE SHEEP

The Bronx, New York. October 1976. Black teenage boys are playing basketball in a playground littered with rubbish. On a nearby street, two men in a black Ford sedan are waiting at a red light. A dump truck is in front of them. The driver of the Ford has already run a red light and a stop sign. He curses impatiently, his fingers drumming on the steering wheel. A surly-looking young man with a shaved head, wearing a shabby army jacket and walking a Rottweiler on a chain leash, comes swaggering around the corner. The two men in the Ford stare at him.

"The fuck you lookin' at?" Shaved Head grunts.

The man in the passenger seat grins behind dark glasses. "Yer ugly mug, cue ball."

"Fuck you!" Shaved Head gives him the finger. The Rottweiler barks, straining at its leash.

The light turns green. The Ford suddenly squeals into reverse, then shoots forward over the curb and slams into the dog, pinning it against a chain-link fence. The two men jump out of the car and attack Shaved Head. They beat him until he slumps to the sidewalk. The dog is yelping and slavering, biting at the chrome bumper. The two men hop into the car and speed off to the funeral of Carlo Gambino – Capo di tutti capi – Boss of all the bosses.

The last time I saw Lenny Filippo he was coming out of the subway station on Dupont Street, in Toronto. That was the fall of 1985. I hadn't seen him in four years. Our chance meeting seemed like a reunion. He was 45 – a year older then me. Although he looked spruce as ever, his hair and beard were grizzled, and there were wrinkles around the outer corners of his eyes. He said he had an appointment with his shrink. "I go three times a week," he added. (I remembered the time I visited Lenny after his second marriage went down the tube, and before he dropped out of sight. He was living like a recluse with three skittish cats in a gloomy apartment that was almost bare of furniture.) I told him my own situation wasn't much better. I was thrice divorced, involved in a hopeless affair with a young married woman, and teaching English part time to computer programming students at a community college in the suburbs. Lenny mentioned he was planning to study analytic psychology at the Jungian Institute of Zurich. I nodded indulgently and wished him good luck. We chatted for a few minutes, shook hands and promised to get in touch, then rushed off in opposite directions.

I first met Lenny in the early 1970s, when he was living with his first wife and two kids in the High Park area of Toronto. Lenny had an imposing look about him. He stood six feet two inches tall and weighed about 190 pounds. Not the kind of guy you'd want to tangle with. His moody disposition was compensated by his sardonic sense of humor. We had certain things in common: we were both first-generation Italians; our sisters had the same first name; our personalities and zodiac signs were compatible. But Lenny's background was more colorful than mine. He was born and raised in the Bronx, New York. He moved to Canada on a student visa to study theology at Assumption College, in Windsor, Ontario, under the tutelage of a Roman Catholic priest who was related to New York's Bishop Fulton J. Sheen. However, Lenny couldn't hack all the religious dogma; so he majored in psychology instead. "My karma ran over my dogma," he was fond of saying.

There was also the fact of Lenny's notoriety among our mutual non-Italian friends. Both Lenny's father and older brother were mafiosi in the New York crime family headed by "Joe Bananas." Lenny didn't advertise this fact. If anything he was bewildered by it, even ashamed.

Although Lenny had been living in Toronto for a decade, he spoke with a Gotham accent. As a lapsed Catholic, he had replaced that faith with the *I Ching* and the psychological doctrines of Carl Jung. He was so hung up on the *I Ching*, he would consult it every morning before going outdoors, wondering if chance was synchronous with fate. He believed that reading Jung helped him in his work as a counselor at a training school for boys. Dreams had a profound effect on him. He fancied himself an oneirocritic, and was convinced that a dream was the mind's distorting mirror in which one's shadow was reflected.

I thought it odd that Lenny had no stomach for crime. He was not only unwilling but morally unable to follow his older brother's example of a loyal mafioso. He once said to me: "I'm the white sheep of my family." He jokingly referred to himself as a "congenital outcast." His marriage to an Anglo-Protestant girl further alienated him from his family. It caused an irreparable break with family tradition, honor and respect. Lenny saw very little of his parents, especially after his father and older brother were caught with a truckload of guns by the RCMP in Montreal. They were both deported from Canada.

Everything is a racket. Lenny remembered his father always trying to impress that kind of philosophy on him. Although Lenny refused to believe in such dark cynicism, it affected his entire outlook on life. As a boy growing up in the crime-ridden Bronx, Lenny got into his share of mischief. Sometimes certain mischief brought the police. There was a shoplifting incident. A store clerk caught Lenny and another boy stealing cigarette lighters. After two policemen checked the boys' ID's, they realized one of them was Vito Filippo's son. With only a warning, they let Lenny go. When a grade-school teacher once asked Lenny what his father did, Lenny said: "He drives around a lot and goes to the opera." Which probably explained Lenny's fondness for the intermezzo in *Cavalleria Rusticana*. He said that listening to it was the only thing that gave him true peace of mind.

A year or so after Lenny's marriage his father's attitude toward him mellowed a bit. He persuaded Lenny, who was unemployed at the time, to move to Las Vegas. Lenny was set up with a well-paying job in a casino – a casino in which his father's boss "Joe Bananas" had a substantial investment. Lenny and his wife (she was asthmatic) enjoyed the hot, dry desert climate. However, he felt out of place in that Mecca of chorus girls and high rollers. He found it too surreal and artificial. "A Disneyland for gamblers," he called it. Most nights police helicopters with blinding, crime-stopper searchlights hovered low over the city. Lenny lasted there six months. He and his wife moved back to Toronto.

Knowing Lenny made me wonder how I'd feel if my own father were a mafioso. Sometimes I played the devil's advocate, and said outrageous things just to gauge Lenny's reaction, and to compare my own moral principles with his. He had a moralistic streak and was very judgmental. I suspected his moral indignation was only jealousy with a halo. He frowned on marijuana (it made him paranoid and belligerent), yet he happily snorted coke if it was offered him. He was funny that way, a real paradox. I was the only person who could get away with teasing him about his upbringing. When we drank together he often told Mafia stories. The Embassy Hotel in Toronto was a favorite hangout of ours.

"What do you get when you cross The Godfather with a lawyer?" Lenny asked me one night.

"I don't know. What do you get?"

"An offer you can't understand."

"Ha-ha. My godfather was Sicilian," I said. "But he was a barber." Since our talk seemed headed in a familiar direction, I said: "Crime is only a left-handed form of human endeavor. Louis Calhern. *The Asphalt Jungle*."

"And every extra dollar has a meaning all its own. Right?"

"Touché. The poor man's Richard Conte." I smiled.

Lenny lit a Gauloises cigarette. "My father had a special way of shaking hands with a person." Extending his hand to shake mine, he demonstrated. "If he was just going through a formality, he'd turn his palm under the other's. But if he accepted the man, he'd shake hands by putting his own palm on top. Something to do with honor. My father thought of himself as a man of honor."

"You always talk about your dad in the past tense, as though he was dead."

Lenny mused for a moment. "Probably because I don't see much of him. He's more a memory than a presence." (I once saw a black-and-white photo of Lenny's dad. He bore a striking resemblance to U.S. Attorney General John Mitchell, when Nixon was president.)

"What about your brother?"

Lenny humphed. "My brother's an arrogant opportunist. He's the only guy I know who can strut while standing still."

I gave a chuckle. "Sibling rivalry?"

"Hardly. Like I said, he's an opportunist with the morals of a lounge lizard."

I took a swig of beer. "Did I ever tell you what happened in the cocktail lounge of the Prince Edward Hotel, in Windsor?"

He shook his head.

"Well, I'm sitting at the end of the bar, nursing a rye and Coke. The stool beside me is empty, and there's an older guy sitting next to it, on my left. This woman walks in – flashy, good-looking, in her thirties – and she asks me if the stool is taken. I tell her no. She smiles, sits down, and orders a martini. And we start making small talk. She's from Chicago. Anyway, I offer her a cigarette, which she takes; and I light it for her. And pretty soon we're getting chummy. I'm also thinking she might be a hooker. She has that look about her. I want to buy her a drink, but I'm low on cash. Anyway, the old guy next to her leaves. And then another guy comes in and sits down on the same stool. The guy looks like the traveling salesman type. He picks up on our conversation, and joins in. I resent his intrusion, but what the hell – he thinks she's with me. Now the woman has two guys entertaining her. After about ten minutes of three-way chitchat, the woman excuses herself and goes to the ladies' room. I can see the guy is quite taken by her; in fact, he can't take his eyes off her. So I ask him – in a low, confidential tone – if he's interested – letting on as though I'm her pimp. His eyes light up. 'I might be. Why?' he says cautiously. Then I tell him that for fifty bucks she'll give him a good half-hour of her time. 'Where?' he asks. Upstairs – in her room, I tell him. He looks at me – all serious and trusting – then pulls out his wallet and hands me two twenties and a ten. She's all yours, I say with a straight face. And I hurry the hell out of there before she comes back."

Lenny laughed. "Just your type: a rich bitch with a rape shape."

"I don't know what got into me. The timing was perfect."

"I wonder what happened."

"Who knows?" I said. "Maybe they hit it off."

Lenny smiled. "You played a Murphy."

"What?"

"A Murphy. A nigger con game played on a white trick."

"You know," I said, "after I got my BCD from the Navy, I still didn't know what to do with my life. My dad was always telling me that I should be either a priest or a gigolo. I used to think he was only joking. It wasn't till I turned thirty that I realized he was serious."

"I guess we both missed our calling," Lenny said, raising his empty beer glass and gesturing to the waiter.

"Yeah, you as a priest, and I as a gigolo. I'll say one thing, though. I respect my dad. I mean, I love him and fear him. And if he ever asked me to kill someone – for whatever reason – I think I would."

"Bullshit!" Lenny scoffed.

"Hey, I mean it! I would. I trust him, and I respect him."

"You're talking through your hat," said Lenny.

The waiter set down four beers.

"No, I'm not. That's how I feel. In this world all you have is your family, provided your family's a good one. Home and family. When you run out of places, isn't home where you go and where they have to let you in? The family's the thing, Lenny. You know that. Look at us. We're first-generation Wops, and we can't even speak Italian except to say *vaffanculo*."

"I think the family's overrated," Lenny said.

"Your dad gave you love, food, shelter . . . "

"What about the sins of the fathers?" he cut in.

"Bible babble. Biology's got us by the balls. The reason you don't believe I'd kill for my dad is because you have a guilt complex about your own dad."

He scoffed. "Sounds like Psychology 101. Don't you have a will of your own?"

"Where there's a will there's a wall," I replied glibly. "Free will's an illusion."

"Has your father ever killed anyone?" he said.

"No."

He gave me a dismissive look. "You should switch to ginger ale. You're beginning to ramble."

"I'm talking about family pride, personal honor, revenge. I remember this movie – *Underworld U.S.A.* Some woman tells Cliff Robertson – 'It was a tough break you had, being born in prison and your mother dying there.' How's that for a start in life? Sometimes I think you're too self-pitying."

"Fuck you!" said Lenny. "Life isn't a film noir."

"No – *vaffanculo*; it sounds better. My dad had a second cousin: Nick Cicchini. He was a small-time crook with big tastes. A regular ladies' man, too. Nick had connections in Detroit. He fenced stolen goods: furs, jewelry, shit like that. But he had delusions of grandeur, and started dealing heroin. One day the RCMP pulled him over on the 401 highway. They found counterfeit money and half a kilo of smack in his car. There was talk an undercover narc had double-crossed him. Poor Nick didn't have enough money for bail. He asked my dad for a loan, but my dad wouldn't give him a dime. Nick broke down and cried like a kid. My dad didn't mind Nick fencing fur coats, but dope was a no-no. When the judge sentenced Nick to twelve years, Nick was so flustered he thanked the judge. Nick was in his late sixties then. He died of a heart attack in Kingston Pen."

"He never would've made it into the Mafia hall of fame," Lenny deadpanned.

We ordered another round of beer.

"On a lighter note," said Lenny, "I remember this guy called Frankie Gloves. A wanna-be mafioso. He did odd jobs for the mob. He always wore gloves – nice kid gloves; wore them indoors, too. He was a burglar who had a fear of his own fingerprints. He used to sandpaper his fingertips. Anyway, the cops picked him up on suspicion of B and E. You know how they identified him?"

"How?"

"They found his shoe-prints in the snow – on the roof of an apartment building."

I laughed, half-choking on my beer.

"There are eight million stories in the naked city," said Lenny. "That was one of them."

"Little Italy must be a bad-ass neighborhood," I said.

"In Manhattan? Are you kidding? It's only a myth wiseguys get shot dead in the streets there. That kind of shit happens more often in Brooklyn and Queens."

"What about Crazy Joe Gallo? Wasn't he murdered in Little Italy?"

"In his case," said Lenny, "an exception was made. Remember Bob Dylan's song about Crazy Joe?"

I nodded. "A nice ballad."

"Yeah. But Dylan romanticized the rubout. Little Italy's a safe place. Nothing but pizza parlors and espresso cafes."

"And private social clubs."

His eyes flashed with irritation. "Why do you get off on romanticizing the Mafia?"

I shrugged.

"So does the fuckin' media; so do most people. They all want a vicarious thrill. Reminds me of my sister. She doesn't like animals, yet she'll wear the skin off a mink's back. And you sounding off on how you'd kill someone if your father told you to. Hah. What a joke."

"You're wrong, Lenny," I said. "That's one of the differences between us."

"Between our fathers, you mean. Most wiseguys are thugs, troglodytes. They wouldn't know a Van Gogh from a Norman Rockwell. A lot of them are functional illiterates. They're arrogant assholes, like my brother: two-faced, ruthless, and paranoid; always looking over their shoulders, sitting with their backs to the wall. None of them has a conscience. They learn how to callus their hearts. I remember this one beast – Sam Scarfone – who lived on my block. He was two years older than me, and in my grade nine class. A mean bastard, always in trouble with the law. He got kicked out of school for stabbing a teacher. After doing time in reformatories and jails, he became a mob enforcer, and collected the vig for loan sharks. They called him 'The Dentist.' If you couldn't pay up, he'd pull out one of your teeth. That was his specialty. Well, his left arm was blown off by a pipe bomb. When FBI agents questioned him in the hospital, he told them to beat it; said he'd get the bastards himself. Anyway, his body was found in the trunk of an abandoned car. He was gagged, his legs were trussed up with wire, and his other arm had been chain-sawed off."

"Hell of a way to go," I said, shuddering.

"He died buckwheats."

"Buckwheats?"

"Yeah. A very painful murder method," said Lenny. "Had the fucker lived, he would've had to use a pair of forceps with his toes. Like I said, the only romantic thing about the Mafia is the music in *The Godfather* movie."

"I saw it twice, then I read the book. Mario Puzo even quoted Balzac: 'Behind every great fortune there's a crime.'"

"What the sociologists don't tell you," said Lenny, "is that eighty percent of human endeavor exists in order to prove that we're better than somebody else."

"Darwin called it survival."

"My father knew a crime boss who had a fancy altar built in the basement of his mansion."

I tittered. "Human sacrifices?"

"No – like in church – so that Mass could be celebrated at family gatherings by a priest." He paused to light a cigarette. "During the Second World War the Vatican asked the Mafia's help in moving tons of silver from an altar in Naples to safety vaults in Rome. And the Mafia obliged them. Seems the Vatican heard the Nazis were going to melt down the silver to pay for their occupation of Italy." He paused again. "Sometimes I think my father was right. Everything *is* a racket."

"Well, to quote my dad: 'Locks were invented to keep honest people honest.'"

"No crime is complete until it's confessed," said Lenny.

We lapsed into thoughtful silence. The hour was late. Both of us were slightly inebriated.

"Hey, *gumbah*," Lenny said suddenly.

"What?"

"*Vaffanculo!*"

When Lenny told me he was going to New York City for a visit, I was surprised. He joked about it: "I'm going there to take a crash course in Mafiaship." The truth was that Lenny and his wife weren't getting along. They both needed some time away from each other. He was leaving a week before the Canadian Thanksgiving. He would be staying with relatives till the end of October.

It so happened that the woman I was living with learned of a Thanksgiving holiday travel package, which included a round-trip flight to New York; accommodations for two nights at a tourist-class hotel; a Broadway play, and a Sunday concert a Lincoln Center. We bought tickets. I hadn't been in New York since 1964, twelve years ago. I mentioned my upcoming trip to Lenny. He gave me his uncle's unlisted phone number. "I'll show you my old stamping grounds," he said.

My lady friend and I flew to the Big Apple. I had no success contacting Lenny. I phoned him several times but there was no answer. Finally, on the last day, a hollow-sounding voice answered my phone call. When I inquired about Lenny, all I got were evasive grunts. It was as though Lenny didn't exist. The telephone operator couldn't even help me.

About two weeks later, I rang up Lenny's wife. She said that Lenny was cutting short his visit and flying home on the 22nd – a Friday. Her tone was brusque. I didn't want to pry. I was still chafing at the rudeness of the creature I'd spoken to when I tried to phone Lenny in New York.

I met Lenny at the Embassy Hotel the night after he got back. He seemed tense, distracted. He ordered a Jim Beam straight, with a Jim Beam chaser. Then he settled down with a pitcher of beer.

"What the hell happened?" I asked outright. "I phoned that number you gave me, and whoever I was talking to sounded like a machine. I couldn't tell whether the voice was a man's or a woman's."

"Yeah, I'm sorry – "

"Wait, listen," I said. "I asked if you were there. *'No. Who's this?'* the voice says, very hollow, as though it was coming from a tomb. I gave my name, and said I was a friend of yours from Toronto. Silence. Then I asked when you'd be in. *'Dunno,'* the voice says. Do you know where he is? I asked. *'No.'* Is he staying at this number? *'No.'* Where can I reach him? *'Dunno.'* Well, if you see him . . .

then the line went dead. I called back, and got a busy signal. Fuck it, I said."

Lenny apologized again. "I got grilled because of your phone call. My uncle kept asking me who you were. I guess your name made him suspicious."

"I should've said Eliot Ness."

"My brother asked me if you knew Paul Volpe." (Volpe was a Toronto mafioso and a friend of Lenny's father.)

"Did you tell them I'm a clean-living bibliophile? Or does rampant paranoia run in your family?"

"Even paranoids have real enemies," said Lenny, unamused.

"The phone was probably bugged anyway. So . . . how was your little vacation?"

"Don't ask. I visited relatives. I met an assortment of hoods. Psychopaths in sharkskin suits. I hung around a few social clubs with my brother. He introduced me to our father's bodyguard. I shook his hand; it felt like bark. Those guys have a language all their own. I overheard some padrone telling a flunky – 'Why don't you put a gun in your mouth and see how many times you can pull the trigger.' A lot of the younger hoods are mainly motivated by moving to the suburbs. I'll say one thing: the Mafia's alive and well."

"No chapter eleven in its future, eh?"

"Hell no! Not when a hood these days can wind up a millionaire. While I was there, Carlo Gambino died. The Big Boss himself. I was at his funeral."

"Really? How'd he die?"

"Old age. The funeral procession was almost a mile long. Tons of flowers. Feds and reporters all over the place; but they were cordoned off from the mourners. The old don went out in *Godfather* style."

"I thought you were staying there till the end of the month."

After a pause, Lenny muttered: "Something changed my mind."

"Like what?"

"I didn't show enough respect."

"Where? At the funeral?"

"No, some club I was in one night. I got drunk and couldn't keep my mouth shut. I was tired of listening to all the bullshit and tough talk; so I made a few sarcastic remarks. I said they all had subpoena envy. They were insulted. It was a serious breach of trust on my part." Lenny paused. He seemed reluctant to continue.

"Well, don't leave me hanging. What happened? Who got insulted?"

"My brother; a few of his buddies. We were in this club. I was a guest. I abused their goodwill. But I was so fuckin' bored with their macho swagger, their talk of scams and money. My brother got pissed off with me. We had a little argument. I made a big mistake trying to show him up in front of his friends. Then he told me he had to split, and would I drive his car home. Hell, I suddenly felt vulnerable. I mean, there I am in a shark tank with guys I have nothing in common, guys I don't even know. I sobered up fast. I wanted to make my exit quickly and quietly as possible. As I was getting ready to leave, two of my brother's gumbahs said they'd go with me. I told them I wasn't drunk, but they insisted."

"Yeah, and – ?"

"So we left. Outside, it was drizzling. We got into my brother's car. One guy's sitting in front; the other one's in back, with his shades on. I'm driving along, and suddenly the guy beside me tells me to pull over. What for? I said. *'Just pull the fuck over,'* he says in a gruff voice. And the guy in the back seat says – *'Do what he tells you.'* So I pull over to the curb. The street's deserted. The guy in front switches off the engine and takes the ignition key.

'*Get out of the car,*' he says. What's going on? I asked. All kinds of crazy thoughts are running through my head. Anyway, all three of us get out of the car. Then before I know what's happening, I get smacked on the side of my head a few times. While I'm getting roughed up by one guy, and trying to protect myself, the other animal grabs my arm and starts talking in my ear." (He mimicked his assailant's voice): "'*Lenny, this is for yer own good. You were way outta line, shootin' off yer yap, actin' like a scumbag.*' It was a weird experience." He took a swig of beer.

I shook my head. "Hell of a homecoming."

"And worst of all – I lost my ring. My thousand-dollar gold wedding band!" He stared dolefully at his left hand, as though his ring finger had been amputated. "It must've come off in the scuffle. They helped me look for it. Imagine that. They kick my ass, and then they help me look for my ring on some filthy sidewalk in the rain. My wife's really ticked off. She's not even speaking to me."

"One of them probably pocketed the thing."

"Yeah, I thought of that," he said bitterly, and gulped down the rest of his beer. "Anyway, when we get to my brother's place, the guy with the shades has the nerve to slap me on the back and say – '*No hard feelings.*' The fuckin' morons."

"What'd your brother say?"

"Nothing. We almost got into a fight."

"Did you tell your dad?"

"Are you kidding?" He looked at me as if I was stupid. "I lost face. I blew it. *Capisci?*"

We were both silent for a few minutes, until Lenny spoke, as if to himself. "If my father finds out . . . "

I ordered another round of beer. On the jukebox Gordon Lightfoot was singing "If You Could Read My Mind."

"I split the next day." He paused, half-smiled, and said:

"On my way to the airport I saw some graffiti on the side of a building. *The light at the end of the tunnel is out.*" He began to laugh unrestrainedly, and then he stopped. "The light at the end of the tunnel is out," he repeated in a muffled voice. There was a look of desolation on his face. The waiter brought us a pitcher of beer. I paid the waiter.

"Forget all that shit," I said, and poured each of us a glass of beer. "Drink up."

He bristled sullenly. For a moment, I thought he was going to take a poke at me. Instead, he picked up his glass and thumped it down on the table, spilling most of the beer. A few customers cast glances in our direction. I looked at him: my friend, my *gumbah* – "the white sheep" who, unlike his gangster father and his older brother, had never married his heaven to his hell, nor his evil to his good.

"What can I say?" I said gently.

"Nothing," he mumbled, trying to contain his agitation. "It's a family matter." He rubbed his face with both hands.

I clinked his glass with mine, and drank. Suddenly he got up from his chair and grabbed his leather jacket.

"Where you going?" I asked in bewilderment.

"Home," he said, and strode toward the door.

Late in 1985 I heard that Lenny Filippo had gone to Switzerland. I presume he went there to study Jungian psychology and to discover his true inner self. I hope he was able to banish his demons and live at peace with his unconscious – not as a moralist but, rather, as a seeker for the truth.

AMY CRISSUM

Rose & Fig Leaf
Tatooing & Expert Cover-Up

reads the sign in the dusty window of a decaying storefront in New Orleans. The storefront studio, long vacant
save for the sign advertising its former occupancy, is on
Frenchmen Street near the French Quarter. "The fringe
of the fringe," the tattooist who plied his trade there used
to say. The tattooist's name was Marc Larose. He lived in
two rooms at the rear of the studio. His bedroom window
looked out on a patch of wild garden in which stood a
sturdy, twenty feet high fig tree.

Marc Larose was a short, wiry Cajun in his early forties.
He had black hair and sported a goatee to compensate for
his receding chin. He walked with a slight limp, the result
of a long-ago Navy accident. His hands were small, delicately boned, and very strong. On his arms and chest were
several tattoos: a chained heart with *Mother* scrolled be-
neath it; a rose, a seahorse, and a pair of balanced scales
– presumably his zodiac sign.

Most people who lived in the vicinity of the Rose &
Fig Leaf regarded Marc Larose as an outsider because of
his glum solitariness. During Marc's five years of shop-
residence on Frenchmen Street he had not made friends
with anyone. Friendship was not a familiar or easy thing
for him. Suspicious and taciturn by nature, he was a lonely,
unsatisfied man. He had never been able to believe that

anybody cared for him. When women treated him tenderly, which sometimes happened in spite of his reserve, he suspected them of deception. He was uncomfortable with women. Consequently his relations with them had been infrequent and brief. Outside of his work his only amusements were fishing and moviegoing. Twice a month he visited his ailing widowed mother in Lafayette.

The truth was that Marc disliked New Orleans. Were it not for his mother who suffered from a debilitating disease, he would have left Louisiana long ago. The thought of moving to the West Coast was always on his mind – until he met a 35-year-old cocktail waitress named Amy Crissum. She got under his skin like a chigger, and gave him an itch and a fever from which he never recovered.

Before Marc opened the Rose & Fig Leaf he earned his living drawing charcoal portraits of people in the mall bordering Jackson Square. Marc had learned tattooing in San Diego, after his medical discharge from the Navy. He was adept at pricking pigment into the skin and making it blossom with vivid designs. Occasionally he got requests for tattoos that were obscene, strange, or crudely humorous. A woman asked him to tattoo an eye on each of her buttocks. Another woman – an Anne Rice freak – had a vampire bat tattooed just below the nape of her neck. Some guy from Boston wanted Marc to duplicate a Matisse line drawing of a satyr and a nymph on his chest. If people were willing to pay money for their fetishes, whims, obsessions, Marc would oblige them. However, he would not do body piercing. That practice was repugnant to him.

It was rumored that Marc could tattoo the soul as well as the skin. The rumor started with a local truck driver. This is what happened. The trucker got a tattoo of a rattlesnake on his leg. Ignoring Marc's advice about giving the finished tattoo a week to dry, the trucker went bayou fishing with his brother-in-law two days later. While fishing, the trucker was bitten on his tattooed leg by a water moccasin. The brother-in-law blabbed the incident. The *Times-Picayune* ran a story headlined: *A SNAKY TWIST*. Marc's name and tattoo parlor were mentioned. The story gave Marc a certain notoriety and helped his business.

Another customer of Marc's – a male stripper nicknamed Angel – experienced a similar fate. A few weeks after Angel was tattooed with blue-and-gold wings, he tested positive for AIDS. Marc was very conscientious about the sanitary appearance of his studio. He used new, sterilized needles for each client.

When Amy Crissum walked into the Rose & Fig Leaf one sultry afternoon in mid-May and asked for a tattoo of a ball and chain on her left ankle, Marc was immediately smitten by her fabulous figure. Amy exuded an unselfconscious friendliness, yet there was streetwise cunning in her demeanor. Her hair was peroxide blonde. She was wearing white capri pants and a deep V-neck tank top. Her cleavage looked bottomless. Her tanned midriff glowed. She had a body which defied all rules and became more seductive because of it. Her waist was round and supple and very slender; below that the white pants clung to thighs and buttocks which were too heavy, as the waist was too slim, but the effect was startling. Even with clothes on she looked naked. In her sandals she stood an inch taller than Marc, who, uncomfortably aware of this fact, avoided standing close to her. They were alone in the studio. The ceiling fan revolved slowly. Irma Thomas was singing "It's Raining" on WWOZ.

Marc was intrigued by Amy's request for a ball-and-chain tattoo. Sensing his curiosity, she drawled: "Jist a reminder to myself not to git hitched agin." She told him she was from Alabama. "Know what an Alabama luau is?"

she said. He shook his head. "Roast possum an' a six-pack." When she laughed, her breasts quivered. "I got tired of strollopin' around 'Bama, so I came down here for Mardi Gras, found me a job, an' this is where I aim to stay."

Tattooing Amy made him nervous. Her perfume was strong, and she oozed sex. It was difficult for him to concentrate on his work. He was glad she did most of the talking. She told him her name, and that she worked at the Blue Dog Café, in the Quarter. (Marc knew the place but had never been there.) She said that she lived on Magazine Street. She also flirted with him a little. He told her he was Cajun, thinking it would impress her; then he tried to make light of it. "As they-all say around here: a *coonass*."

"I love Cajun food, crawdads an' all," she said.

"Pinch da tails an' suck da heads," he said.

She chuckled. "Say something Cajun."

He smiled shyly, stopped his tattooing, and thought for a moment.

"Oh, come on," she begged. "I never heard anyone talk Cajun."

"*Pendant la nuit, tous les chats sont gris,*" he said suddenly.

She squealed with delight. "What's that mean?"

"At night, all cats are dark."

"Ain't that the truth," she said.

It wasn't long before Marc started going to the Blue Dog Café. The place was mostly patronized by tourists, and it served mediocre but pricey Cajun and Creole cuisine: crawfish *etouffee*, gumbo, jambalaya. Zydeco music played nonstop. On the walls of the café were framed prints of George Rodrigue paintings, Mardi Gras posters, and big red plastic crawfish. Marc hated the hyped-up Cajun ambience, the fake charm, the Yankee tourists who thought they were having a unique cultural experience. Marc would sit at a corner table if one was available, or at the bar, drinking bourbon. Amy was usually too busy to chat with him. She seemed to enjoy her work. She bantered with the male customers, and they gave her generous tips. Once he overheard some loudmouthed drunk ask her if she was a waitress. "No, but I play one on TV," she deadpanned. Marc felt like an intruder at the Blue Dog Café.

Marc wanted desperately to be alone with Amy, but he was too timid to ask her out. He hadn't slept with a woman in almost two years. Sometimes he tormented himself with imaginary doubts and fears, and fell prey to a psychic impotence of which he was ashamed. Amy sensed his lack of assertiveness, and took advantage of it by teasing him. The bartender at the Blue Dog Café sized up Marc right away: "He's like a dog with a harelip. *Mark, mark, nark!*"

Amy was pleased with her tattoo. The ball and chain, however, did not restrict her sexual activities. If a man interested her, she went to bed with him. Men were attracted to her, and she knew it. It was as though she gave off an aphrodisiac scent. When she was only thirteen, she remembered her mother telling her father: "Amy's growed too fast. She's got man-fever." Because Marc didn't physically excite her, she kept him dangling.

After two weeks of seeing Amy at the Blue Dog Café, and phoning her on her days off, Marc was finally rewarded for his doglike devotion. One misty evening Amy invited Marc to supper at her place. "Nothin' fancy," she said. "Jist catfish stew an' greens."

The courtyard was shabby and paved with bricks. A broken, moss-covered fountain stood in the center, and an outside stairway led to the roofed wooden gallery which ran all the way around the second storey. The odor of damp vegetation filled Marc's nostrils as he climbed the steps. Wet vine leaves brushed his face. He crushed a large cockroach underfoot. He was holding a bottle of red wine in one hand and a long-stemmed red rose in the other. Halfway down one side of the gallery was Amy's apartment. He rapped on the door. He waited a moment, and then he rapped again.

"Jist a sec!" Amy called out. Through a torn window screen he could hear country music.

The door opened. "Sorry. I was in the shower," Amy said.

He handed her the rose, and apologized for being early. She pecked him on the cheek. She was wearing a pink taffeta housecoat, and she was barefoot. Her hair was wet; she kept dabbing at it with a towel. He noticed some dark roots showing.

"Scuse the muss," she said, picking up a pair of jeans from the sofa. "Make yourself comfy. I gotta dry this hair an' fix my face. There's beer in the fridge. I won't be but a minute."

The small front room was untidy. Marc looked for a place to sit down. There were strings of Mardi Gras beads everywhere. The carpet had stains and cigarette burns. Clothes, unwashed glasses, shoes, magazines, wadded Kleenex tissues littered the room. On top of the portable TV was a marabou slipper with a three-inch heel. His eyes scanned the room for the slipper's twin. He lit a cigarette, and noticed the ashtray on the coffee table was spilling over with ashes and cigarette butts. Some of the filters were lipstick-stained. He was both surprised and disappointed she hadn't bothered to tidy up. He wasn't put off by her slovenliness; rather, it affected him in an obscurely erotic way. The subtropic heat and humidity made the small apartment a throbbing blood-temperature. The aroma of catfish stew hung in the air. He was sweating, his clothes felt sticky. He wondered why the ceiling fan was off. As he was trying to switch it on, Amy came out of the bathroom and walked into the front room.

"The fan's on the blink," she said. "I bin after the landlord to fix it." Her face was made up, she had blow-dried her hair. She was still in her housecoat.

"You look lovely, Amy," he said. "The beautifulest – of any woman."

She smiled and stood close to him. He suddenly put his arm around her but she pulled away. "You're right frisky," she said. "Let's have a drink of wine, the stew ain't near ready."

They sat in the kitchen, drinking wine and smoking. Marc was so aroused by the way she kept crossing and uncrossing her legs, giving him a glimpse of her smooth round thighs, that he could hardly make conversation. She slid her foot up and down his shin. They had almost finished the bottle of wine, and she hadn't mentioned dinner yet. Not that he cared, though he noticed the sink was piled with dirty dishes. When she deliberately nudged his groin with her foot, he grabbed the foot and began kissing it.

"Stop it! Don't! It tickles!" she laughed, wiggling in her chair. Her housecoat came undone, but she made no effort to cover herself.

Seeing his chance, he released her foot, and in one quick motion was at her – kissing her mouth, her neck, her hair, mumbling – "Amy, I love you – Amy, I love you!"

She drew her mouth from his. "What about the fish stew?" she said coyly.

He could tell she was slightly drunk. "Let it stew – " he mumbled, slavering over her breasts.

"No sense us sittin' here," she said, and got up from her chair. She shut off the electric stove, then glided toward the bedroom. "Comin'?" she leered at him, letting her housecoat slide to the floor.

The bedroom was messy and the bed unmade. On the dresser a small fan was blowing tepid air. The rose he'd given her was sticking out of a Dixie beer bottle on the night table. He undressed hurriedly. The moment he embraced her soft, luscious body he knew this was something outside his experience.

"Do anything you want," she said.

He was so overexcited that within seconds of entering her, he ejaculated.

"Don't stop! Give it to me! Fuck me hard!" she yelled and wiggled, digging her fingernails into his buttocks.

With all his might he tried to maintain his erection. She came again and again, twice ejecting him over her heaving.

"Stick it in my big butt!" she urged him. "I like it both ways."

When Marc awakened, the morning sunlight was bright on the floor and on the big waxy leaves of the magnolia outside the unshuttered window. He could hear a mockingbird singing. Amy was asleep. He remembered going to the bathroom in the middle of the night. He had peeked in her medicine cabinet and found several condoms. He wondered why she hadn't asked him to wear one. The condoms made him think of her having sex with other men. He felt a stab of jealousy. To dispel the unbidden images, he thought of her slovenliness and of the cockroaches he'd seen in her kitchen. But certain telltale things (a man's leather belt under a pillow) fretted on his mood. His penis was painfully stiff. He had to urinate; yet he lay there, gazing at her body on the rumpled bedsheet . . . the swell of her hip . . . her white round buttocks. He grasped his penis and jerked it a little, and then he began playing with it. He wanted to stick it into her while she was sleeping. He wanted to do the other thing, too. She said she liked it both ways. He touched her cunt. It was still wet from last night. He smelled his fingers. She stirred in her sleep. He'd show her how virile he was. He'd pleasure her all day. Propping himself on one elbow, he suddenly noticed a silver-mounted photograph on a low table in the corner. It was the face of a child – a girl – about ten years old. He thought it strange the child wasn't smiling. In fact the child looked sad.

Marc was enthralled by Amy. Determined to have her all to himself, he courted her with a singleness of purpose. He altered his work hours to accommodate hers. He catered to her whims and was receptive to her moods. He flattered her, wined and dined her at fancy restaurants, chauffeured her to the beauty salon, bought her flowers, jewelry, and lent her money which she seldom paid back. He couldn't do enough for her. It was as if his life had now taken on the vivid colors of his tattoos. For the first time he felt happy. He walked with less of a limp. Yet he would sulk when she wore high heels. He would become indignant when other men ogled her.

To become the aggressor in a relationship is to forfeit an advantage. By showing Amy how much he wanted and needed her, in revealing his own weakness, uncertainty, and inexperience with women, Marc unwittingly placed himself in a situation in which he was both dominated and manipulated. Amy saw and felt his weakness, his possessiveness; and because of her sexually promiscuous nature plus the fact she didn't love him, she was in a position to chart the course of their relationship in any way she chose.

Marc had only a sketchy knowledge of Amy's background. He knew she'd been married twice, and that she had a mentally retarded daughter who lived in Alabama with Amy's mother. (Another daughter had been given away for adoption.) He also knew Amy had been raped by her stepfather when she was thirteen; and that she had worked briefly as a stripper. However, he didn't know Amy was still legally married. He didn't know the Alabama Family Services had charged her with child abandonment and endangerment. Nor did he know she had performed in a porn film. Amy related one tragic incident for which she felt partly responsible. It happened when she was 16. Her mention of it was triggered by some racial slur Marc made.

Amy was fond of a black boy in the small town where she lived. The boy was her age. He was handsome and very popular with the black girls. One afternoon Amy and the boy were seen necking in the woods by three white men who were squirrel hunting. All three men were in their twenties. They roughed up the boy, and called Amy a "nigger lover." A few days later the same three men abducted the boy and took him in their car to an abandoned barn. They gave the boy a savage beating, and then they cat-hauled him. Two of the men held the boy on the ground while the third fetched a stray cat from the trunk of their car. The cat was taken by the tail and forcibly dragged along the boy's bare back, its claws ripping flesh all the way. Then they tied the boy's hands behind his back with some binder twine, and threw him into a creek that was notorious for its population of snapping turtles. The boy drowned. A week later the three men were picked up by the police, held overnight in jail, and then released. The youngest of the three was the sheriff's nephew. Amy neglected to tell Marc that she went to a motel with the sheriff's nephew a month after the murder.

In late June, Amy moved her belongings (mostly clothes) to the Rose & Fig Leaf. Marc was elated; his mind whirled at the prospect of sleeping with Amy every night. Although he knew from past experience that nothing equaled the cruelty of a woman if she despised a man, he now wondered if the goodness of women was only an illusion, and what they really valued in men were primitive virtues, like strength and energy. He did not know that Amy's landlord had evicted her.

A week after her move, Amy went from working full time to part time. At first Marc was pleased. ("I can support both of us," he told her.) Then he began to fret. During the day Amy was seldom at the studio. She made shopping and other errands a pretext for rendezvousing with the occasional conventioneer in his hotel room. She had to exercise caution and duplicity though. Sometimes Marc wheedled her into telling her whereabouts at a certain time of day. Because he had a fetish for lingerie, Amy would allay his suspicion by modeling a new see-through bra or a garter belt for him. "I bought this little bitty thing at Victoria's Secret. Don't you jist love it?"

On her days off, Amy usually slept till noon. "My lazy slut sleep," she called it. Other than making chicory-flavored coffee or boiling grits, she rarely cooked. Her efforts at keeping the studio clean were halfhearted. Yet Marc tolerated her laziness. Because he lacked a sense of humor, Amy said and did things which caught him off guard and caused him to feel insecure about their relationship. On one occasion he sulked for a whole day over some critical remark she made about his lovemaking.

Several nights a week Marc and Amy went out to hear live music at the Maple Leaf Bar, Tipitina's, and other clubs. Amy loved to dance. She knew how to use her body to music. Marc tagged along reluctantly. He did not dance very well. His graceless shuffling on the dance floor reminded Amy of "someone trying to scrape dogshit off his shoes."

One Friday night, at the Maple Leaf Bar, Marc spotted his favorite movie actress, Kathleen Turner. He had read in the *Times-Picayune* that Kathleen Turner was working on location in New Orleans. With the actress was some man. Marc thought the man looked unimpressive beside her. She was taller and more hefty than him.

They were all watching Rockin' Dopsie Jr. and his band, The Zydeco Twisters, sweating their way through a hot, high-spirited set. The Maple Leaf Bar was crowded, smoky, and jumping. Marc kept glancing at the actress. He was standing only a few yards away from her.

"That's Kathleen Turner! . . . the movie star," Marc whispered to Amy, nodding toward the actress.

Amy shrugged. "So what? She looks fat." Her tone betrayed surprise and resentment. It was the first time she had seen Marc admiring another woman, and it piqued her. "Why don't you ask her for a dance?" she said loudly and mockingly. Marc looked away. "Go on, ask her." She nudged him. "Tell her you're a big fan of hers."

Just then a man with a short ponytail and a gold earring glided up to Amy, indicating he wanted to dance with her. He smiled slyly. Although there was no greeting, Marc had the feeling that the man and Amy knew each other. At once she began dancing with him.

The music ended, and another rousing number started up. Amy danced with the man again. Some of her moves became provocative and wanton. Marc was embarrassed. The man was clasping Amy's hips. They were doing the belly rub. Marc glared at them. He wished he had the nerve to ask Kathleen Turner for a dance. Upset, he sidled over to the bar and ordered a beer. He gazed blankly at the people dancing. He wished the loud music would stop. Jealousy welled up in him. He finished his beer, and ordered a Sazerac for Amy. He eased his way back through the crowd. He couldn't find Amy. Confused, he prowled about the barroom but couldn't find her anywhere. He lingered by the door to the ladies' room. A few women gave him amused looks. He felt foolish. He gulped down the Sazerac, and then he went outside to cool off. He was boiling with indignation.

A half-hour later Amy found Marc sitting in his car, glowering. She climbed unsteadily into the car, a plastic go-cup of beer in her hand. "I bin lookin' all over for you," she said, spilling some of the beer on her skintight jeans.

Marc scowled. "Who was that *couillon*? Your old boy-friend?" (He often lapsed into Cajun dialect when he was excited or angry.)

"No. We were jist dancin'. Then we had a drink," she said.

"*Chu de cochon!* He looked like a fag. Did you have time to fuck him?"

"You got no call accusin' me – "

"He was feelin' up your ass, an' you love it."

"We were dancin', gittin' down. Goddamnit, Marc, act like you're somebody."

"*I am somebody!* I ain't no gui-gui from the swamps. What are you, eh?"

"Want me to git a taxi?" she threatened, opening the door.

He could tell she was drunk. "No. We should go home," he muttered, and started the car.

"Here. Cool your jets." She handed him her beer. He took a swig, then tossed the go-cup out the window and drove off.

By the time they reached Canal Street, they were quar-reling again. When Marc stopped for a traffic light, Amy suddenly opened the door on her side of the car, stepped out into the street, slammed the door behind her and walked away. As soon as the light changed, Marc pulled over to the curb, cut the engine, and ran after her.

"Amy! Wait!" he called out.

Amy stood on the curb, waiting to cross the street. "Go away!" she said. "I don't like bein' called a liar."

"I just wanted for you to tell the truth," Marc said. "Why say I called you a liar?"

"C'mon, Marc, don't piss on my back an' tell me it's rainin'," she lashed at him. "You're jist jealous."

He was standing in the gutter, looking up at her beseechingly. It struck him how short and ridiculous he looked. She seemed aware of it, too. He stepped onto the curb. "Please come back in the car," he said softly. He took hold of her arm, but she jerked it away.

"Leave me alone! I feel like walkin'. I need some time to myself." She dashed halfway across Canal Street, waited for a streetcar to pass, then trotted to the other side and disappeared into the French Quarter.

Marc drove home in a deep funk. An hour later he lay in bed, waiting for Amy, trying to numb his anxiety with bourbon and a joint. He stared up at the pale green ceiling, at the spidery cracks in it. The longer he stared at the cracks, the more they seemed to form the outlines of a headless woman, with her legs crossed, masturbating a headless man. He wondered why he hadn't noticed the two headless figures before.

He was still awake when Amy came in at four in the morning. She undressed in the dark and then got into bed. He imagined he smelled the aftermusk of sex on her. She fell asleep almost at once. He lay awake for a while, and finally fell asleep himself.

In the muggy, ninety-plus degree heat, the mockingbirds were silent. Only the cicadas sang. Their steady high-pitched hum seemed to swell from the ground, the trees, and even from the skies, till the air itself throbbed with sound. The humidity hung thick as Spanish moss.

One morning in late July Amy told Marc she was pregnant. She told him matter-of-factly, without emotion. "My last period was in May," she added, "when I got my tattoo."

Marc was stunned. It meant she was two months pregnant. "Why didn't you tell me sooner?" he said.

"I don't know. I wasn't sure," Amy said. "It must've happened the night I made us catfish stew."

Marc had mixed feelings about this new situation. Had she seen a doctor yet? Amy told him not to worry, she would get an abortion. Her mention of the word put his thoughts in a knot. Even though he was a lapsed Catholic, he was against abortion. What if it was his? What if it wasn't? Trust and doubt struggled for truth. He reckoned he would have to accept on faith the truth it was his. His faith was motivated by the knowledge he loved her. Amy told him she would have the baby if that was what he wanted.

Two weeks later, Marc's mother died. Marc was devastated by grief and guilt. His mother's death seemed to him a sign of rebuke. Since becoming involved with Amy he had neglected to visit his mother. Now his mother's funeral arrangements pressed upon his mind.

It was only a two-hour drive to Lafayette, and Marc felt compelled to go there at once. Knowing he'd be away for a few days, he asked Amy if she wanted to go with him. She begged off, saying that she had to sub for one of the waitresses who was ill. Her selfishness and lack of grace hurt him. His hurt was exacerbated by the fact he loved her but did not trust her. As for his nervous ambivalence toward her pregnancy, he tried to convince himself it would strengthen their relationship, and he took some comfort in that.

After the funeral, and late in the evening, Marc headed back to New Orleans. He had been gone three days. During that time he got maudlinly drunk, quarreled with his married sister over their mother's will, and mulled over Amy's pregnancy. He had phoned Amy at least a dozen times, left loving messages in his voice mail, but spoken to her only twice. As he tooled along Interstate 10, his mood wavered between anxiety and desire. He nearly hit an armadillo, dead on the highway.

Outside Baton Rouge Marc got a speeding ticket. When he reached the sprawling suburb of Metairie, he exited off the interstate and stopped at the first phone booth he saw. He rang the Blue Dog Café. Amy wasn't there. A glance at his wristwatch showed almost nine-thirty. Amy wasn't expecting him till the next day. He wanted to surprise her.

The Rose & Fig Leaf was in darkness except for a light in the bedroom window. Impulsively Marc went around to the back door. It was then he heard a succession of short muffled cries followed by a man's husky voice: *"Whip it on her!"*

Marc froze; his mouth went dry. He slowly backed away from the door, his heart racing. He stood motionless under the shadow of the large fig tree, staring up at the lighted, moth-flecked window screen. A sudden breeze from the river rustled the leaves of the tree, which stood opposite the window. Carefully he hoisted himself up the tree. Crouching forward on a thick branch and using his hands for support, he had the aspect of a gargoyle.

Amy lay in bed, sandwiched between two black men who were having vaginal and anal sex with her.

Marc's face blanched with horror. He shuddered. A twig snapped off in his hand. He tensed, his ears pounding with the silent roar of his blood rage. He wished he had his .38. But he was too unnerved to do anything. With some difficulty he climbed down the tree, and slinked out of the yard. On Esplanade Avenue, where his car was parked, he vomited.

At K&B Drugs he bought a pint of Early Times. Then he drove to the Garden District, parked on a quiet, magnolia-lined street, and drained the pint in three gulps. Lurid sex images and thoughts of murder kept him awake all night.

The morning sky was overcast. Marc had a raging headache. He felt clammy. He struggled through the morning, did some banking and took care of a few small business matters.

When he arrived at his studio, it was near noon. Amy was in the shower. He sat down wearily, and lit a cigarette. The thought of seeing her face sickened him.

Presently Amy stepped out of the bathroom, a towel wrapped around her. She gave a little start of surprise when she saw him. "I didn't hear you come in," she said. "You look like you bin rode hard an' put up wet. How was the funeral?"

Marc grunted, without looking at her.

"I missed you," she said, and leaned down to kiss him. He turned away. "Well, somebody came back all grumpy."

He told her the funeral depressed him. He lit another cigarette.

"I got the day off," she said. "Why don't we do something special?"

"A special surprise I have for you," he muttered, and cleared his throat. "But not till tonight."

Her face brightened. "I got something to show you right now. It'll chase away your blues." She went into the bedroom.

He sat there, willing his countenance back to composure. A minute later she pranced out, wearing a rose-pink teddy, and posed for him. "Well? Do you like it?"

He nodded but said nothing. Desire and repulsion were so fused in him, he could not distinguish one from the other. His impassivity perplexed her. She pouted a little.

"I'm not in the mood for dress-up," he said. "Tonight will be different." He forced a smile. "A nice surprise I have – just for you." He told her that he had to take his car in for a tune-up, and that he would be back at six. On the door of his studio he hung a *CLOSED* sign.

Her vanity pricked, Amy spent the afternoon watching soap operas, painting her toenails, getting stoned, and dozing off.

By late afternoon it was dark, with thunderclouds massing in the eastern sky. As soon as Marc walked in the door, he could smell pungent marijuana smoke. Amy was curled up on the sofa, in her housecoat. The TV was on. She greeted him languidly. "Looks like it's gonna rain," she half-yawned.

"Let it rain black cats," he said, and switched off the TV.

"If you're hungry, there's some leftover red beans an' rice. Or we could order a pizza." She smiled indolently.

"Let me fix you a drink first," he said, and went into the kitchen. He opened a can of beer, and took a few swigs. And then he made a Sazerac, with extra bourbon.

She took a sip of her cocktail. "I swear you make the best Sazerac," she said, and took another sip. "Well, where's my surprise?"

"Not now. In a bit." He turned on the radio.

She smiled. "You know, Marc, I think bein' pregnant makes me feel more sexy."

He winced as though in pain.

"Not that you really care – " she said petulantly.

"Let me get you a refill."

She jiggled the ice in her glass. "Sure. Why not?"

He took her glass and left the room.

"I feel like I'm about ready to jist float away," she called out, stretching her arms.

From an eyedropper he squeezed two grams of chloral hydrate into her Sazerac. There were heavy peals of thunder.

"A little *lagniappe*," he said, handing her the drink. "Then you can have your surprise."

She took a sip, and made a face. "It tastes bitter."

"Because your lips are so sweet, *ma chere*."

"Am I still the *beautifulest*?"

"Yes, the only one." He sat down beside her.

It began to rain heavily. A cloudburst. She nestled her shoulder close against him.

"I jist love it when it rains," she said, then yawned. "That Irma Thomas song about the rain. How does it go?" She tried to hum the melody, but her voice was slightly off-key.

Her speech gradually became slurred; she yawned often. Finally she drifted into a drugged sleep. Marc lifted her eyelids to make sure she was unconscious. On the radio, Muddy Waters was singing "Hoochie-Coochie Man." The song spurred him to action. He stretched Amy out lengthwise on the sofa, undid her housecoat, and placed a small cushion under her lower back. Then he got his tattooing instruments and set to work, tracing a design on her smooth belly, the electric needle whirring in his hand. He was nervous and sweaty. "I'm the hoochie-coochie man," he said, and then he chanted:

> *"I got a black cat bone,*
> *I got a mojo too,*
> *I got the John the Conqueroo,*
> *I'm gonna mess with you . . . "*

He hummed, he whistled, he sang. "Yeah, bitch, I'm gonna mess with you. I'm gonna ball an' chain your ass for good."

It took Marc two hours to finish the tattoo. It wasn't one of his better efforts, but he was satisfied with the result. On Amy's belly was the tattoo of an erect, blue-black phallus – about seven inches in length – and plum-sized testicles. The phallus curved diagonally, its glans terminating at her navel. Amy's breathing made the tattoo seem alive.

It was a quarter past ten. It was still raining. Marc began quickly packing his things. When he had finished loading his car, he went into the bedroom. On top of the dresser lay a red garter belt. He thrust it into the pocket of his raincoat. Then he spat on the unmade bed. On his way out he paused to look at Amy sprawled on the sofa. *"Salope!"* he hissed.

Marc had already decided on California as his destination. By the time Amy came to, he would be halfway to Texas.

"Laissez le bon temps rouler," Marc muttered to himself as he drove away.

THE SUCCUBUS

That fende that goth a nyght,
Wymmen full oft to gyle.
Incubus is named by ryght;
And gyleth men other whyle,
Succubus is that wyght.

Caxton's *Cronycle*

Lillian was troubled by the fact that after three years of marriage her husband Roger no longer desired her. She suspected it had something to do with her recent hysterectomy. The few times she brought up the matter with Roger, he gave her a little hug and told her she was over-reacting. Lillian couldn't remember the last time they had made love. It was as if Roger had imposed a moratorium on their lovemaking without her consent.

Although Lillian tried to reconcile her own ideals of love with the passionless reality of her situation, the memory of their past intimacy now intensified her loss. She was frustrated, she felt unloved – and feeling unloved, she blamed her body, as most women do. She was Roger's third wife. He was her second husband. A year after their marriage they had moved, on Roger's insistence, from Toronto to Vancouver. With them was Lillian's sexually precocious 15-year-old daughter, Jenny.

Love is only a sublimation of the libido, was Roger's pet paraphrase of Freud whenever the subject of relations between the sexes came up in conversation. Roger was in his middle forties. He taught language arts to adult students four evenings a week. He was also "writing a novel." A euphemism, thought Lillian, for his selfishness and irresponsibility.

At 40, Lillian considered herself attractive but overweight. She was always dieting but never seemed to lose a pound. Tofu, bean sprouts, cottage cheese and salads were dull substitutes for candlelight dinners. "Junoesque" was how Roger proudly described her when they were first married. Most of a woman's beauty is derived from her belief in that beauty. Roger's nagging at her plumpness shattered that belief. Lillian was painfully aware that her waistline, which once emphasized her voluptuous hips, now made her look unshapely. Her clothes were getting tighter. A few varicose veins had begun to show on her calves. There was cellulite on her buttocks and thighs. As her depression grew, so did her indulgence in sweets. She was further frustrated when she found out Jenny was smoking marijuana.

Because Lillian was quiet, a good listener, and inclined to prudent restraint in the expression of opinions, her modesty was often mistaken for meekness. On the other hand, her sensual nature seemed to exemplify the proverbial "still waters run deep." It was her deep, quiet sensuality that had initially captivated Roger. Lillian was resourceful as well. She worked in the office of a busy catering firm. In a sense, she was the real breadwinner.

Jenny hated her mother's submissive demeanor, her mushy sentimentality. They were complete opposites in temperament. Jenny was willful and sassy. Before puberty Jenny used to curl up innocently in Roger's lap. Now she was coquettish with him only to spite her mother. The fact she had a nubile figure and dressed like a little tart put Roger in a delicate position. Lillian was so caught up in her own emotional needs that she neglected her daughter's. Jenny remembered the traumatic circumstances of her first menstruation, which happened several months after her mother and Roger were married.

Jenny woke up one morning, saw blood on her nightgown, and scrambled out of bed. In her fearful excitement she burst into her mother's bedroom without knocking. The sight of Roger's bare buttocks, and her mother lying under him, moaning, with her legs cocked in the air, stunned her. What humiliated Jenny wasn't Roger's startled curse but her mother's servile apology to him. Jenny never forgave her for that.

Roger had been twice unfaithful to Lillian: with a divorcee, and with one of his students – a Jamaican nanny. Yet he felt no guilt. Lillian's jealousy and self-abasement disgusted him more. She would fawn over him in front of Jenny, and make a fool of herself. Roger was so bored with his marriage, that he had to psych himself up to have sex with Lillian. He would fantasize that Jenny was peeking at them while he mounted Lillian from behind – silently, grimly, mechanically – until she climaxed. On one such occasion she became tearful afterwards, and sniveled: "Why can't we always be like this?" He didn't know what to say.

With his wife at work and Jenny at school, Roger had the weekdays to himself. He enjoyed being alone in their apartment on 18th Avenue near Cambie Street. If he didn't have a book to review or papers to mark, or he wasn't in the mood to work on his novel, he would smoke a joint and daydream. One rainy day in late September, while correcting his students' compositions and fortifying himself with vodka and grapefruit juice for that tedious task, he got up from the chair to stretch his legs and suddenly felt dizzy. He wandered about the apartment, looking for distractions. His steps took him toward Jenny's bedroom. The door was closed. He couldn't resist the impulse to open it. Snooping around in her bedroom while she was at school seemed an obscene violation of her privacy. As always, her room was untidy, her bed unmade. The walls were covered with garish posters of rock musicians. Shoes, dirty socks, underthings, teen magazines, a paperback novel by Stephen King, costume jewelry, souvenirs were scattered about. A wire mobile with metal fish hung from the ceiling above her bed. He flicked it with his hand, setting it in motion. In a half-open bureau drawer he found a roach clip. In another drawer, buried under some lingerie, was a folded, three-page letter. There was no envelope. The letter had a recent date but no address, and was neatly handwritten on lavender paper. *Dear Jenny*, it began. He was about to put it back when a certain clause caught his eye: *so we took off our clothes.* He read on. *The thing was we didn't have much time. The people I was baby-sitting for told me they'd be back at midnight. Anyway, we were kissing, and his hands were touching me all over, and pretty soon we got down to where there wasn't anything to do but you know what – and we did THAT!* He read further, but there were only references to school and rock music. The letter was signed – *Your friend, Donna,* accompanied by several *X's* and a *PS* that read: *Don't worry; I'm on the pill.* He replaced the letter carefully, then left the room, shutting the door behind him. The letter had aroused him. He thought of Jenny in her white, one-piece, spandex bathing suit. He imagined her sitting in his lap, laughing and wriggling as he tickled her in the ribs and held her firmly around her slender waist. He wondered if she was still a virgin. Boys were always phoning her. If she were 17, he might be tempted to run away with her. They would drive across Canada. A motel odyssey – *a mari usque ad mare.* He thought of the film *Lolita,* and tried to picture Lillian as the blowsy, outraged mother, and himself as the bookish, nymphet-obsessed stepfather. When he returned to his desk he found it impossible to concentrate. He sat brooding, watching the rain stir the large leaves of the horse-chestnut tree outside his window. He decided that he would leave his wife.

That night Roger had a disturbing dream. He was walking along a leaf-strewn sidewalk in a residential neighborhood late at night. The neighborhood looked unfamiliar to him. The tree-lined street was deserted, all the houses were dark. A damp wind rattled the branches of trees. He could hear the susurrus of leaves as they fell and blew away, skittering over the front yards and along the street. There were leaves everywhere. Under the street-lamps they shone yellow, brown, red. His shoes shuffled through them. Suddenly he saw a black cat. It was sitting on the edge of a wide, white veranda. He stopped to look at the cat. The cat gazed at him, its amber eyes glowing. He called to it, making soft, squeaking sounds by pursing his lips. The cat neither moved nor meowed. He moved on. After walking fifty feet or so, he glanced over his shoulder. The cat, a large sleek one, was now standing on the sidewalk in front of the verandaed house. Surprised, he stopped and called to it again. But it just stood there. He turned and continued walking. Then he looked back again. The cat *had moved*, as though it was stalking him. It looked larger than before. Intrigued, he stopped, meowed softly, made sibilant sounds, and gestured with his hands, trying to coax it closer. The cat remained motionless, its tail held low. Impatient, he resumed walking till something made him look back. The cat *was* following him. It looked larger still. But when he stopped, it stopped too. He waited, then took a few steps toward it. It hissed at him. He stopped, turned around and hurriedly walked away. When he reached the corner of the street he looked back once more. The cat had grown even larger. Its dark shadow stretched toward him . . .

He woke up with a start. His legs and back felt stiff. Beside him Lillian stirred in her sleep. The clock radio on the night table showed 4:11 a.m. The dream still gripped him; he couldn't get back to sleep. He eased himself out of bed, went to the kitchen, drank a glass of tapwater, then sat down in the living room and smoked a cigarette. The strange dream had spooked him. He seldom dreamed, or if he did, he could never remember them on waking. Trying to interpret dreams seemed to him a waste of time. He had no interest in oneiromancy. He believed that dreams were an almost mystic language to which he did not hold the key. In any case, he was fond of cats. He had dipped into enough volumes of forgotten lore to know that the cat was an archetypal image of the feminine principle and the anima, and that cats played an extensive part in the mythology of female supernatural beings. He told Lillian and Jenny about his dream. Jenny said it was "awesome."

Three nights later Roger had another dream – an erotic dream that culminated in an orgasm. He not only felt pleasurably relieved but was even more amazed by the experience itself. He couldn't remember when he'd last had a wet dream. He wondered if the vitamin E capsules, damiana capsules and expensive yohimbine tablets he took almost daily were finally having an effect on him. Lillian was upset. His dream awakened her. Although he tried to conceal the spots of semen on the bedsheet, she felt the sticky wetness against her leg. "I guess you're denying me sex so you can get it in your sleep," she grumbled. "I hope whoever she was satisfied you." She got out of bed in a huff, and went to sleep on the sofa.

The woman in his dream was someone he had never seen before. Of that he was certain. Had she been an ex-wife, a former girlfriend, or some pickup he remembered bedding, he might have given no further thought to the matter. The fact she was unknown to him filled him with wonderment. He pondered the intimate connection between erotic wishes and psychological repression. As a teenager, he'd had masturbatory fantasies of Jayne Mansfield. Fantasizing was controllable. To be a plaything of the unconscious was an adventure. In his dream, he remembered the woman was naked save for a red beret that crowned her head like a halo. Long, dark hair cascaded down over her shoulders. She wore bright red lipstick, and her eyes were heavy-lidded, almost half-closed. Her body was slim and supple. She hardly spoke but rather abandoned herself to him in a delirious, half-forgetting passion. He also remembered there was an infant squalling in a crib.

One night Roger surprised his wife by making love to her. It happened while Jenny was having a slumber party. The sight of Jenny laughing and frolicking with her two girlfriends aroused him. For their sake, he retired to his bedroom. When Lillian came in to put on her nightgown, he was lying in bed, leafing through one of her *Cosmopolitan* magazines. "Sounds like they're having a good time," he said to her, tossing the magazine on the floor. "Close the door and stay awhile." She could tell from his tone of voice and the look on his face that he was horny. It was the last time they had sex together.

A week later, Roger dreamed of the dark-haired woman again. The physical surroundings in his dream were shadowy, phantasmagoric. He and the woman were sitting in the backseat of a hearse. His second ex-wife was driving, and she kept glancing at him in the rearview mirror. The woman's hand was inside his fly. Then he noticed the hearse's windows had turned into mirrors, and the hearse was moving backwards. Suddenly he was in a dimly lit room. He could hear the tinkling of wind chimes. He was locked in a *soixante-neuf* embrace with the dark-haired woman. She lay on top of him. His face was buried in the cleft of her buttocks, which swelled and contracted rhythmically like two halves of a huge inverted heart. He woke up with a throbbing erection, unsure whether he was awake or still dreaming, wondering where the woman had vanished.

So bewitched was Roger by the dark-haired woman, that he attempted to write some verses on the phenomenon. Who was she? Her face was unfamiliar to him. She didn't remind him of any woman he'd ever known. He had a vague notion she might be a phantasm of his own imagination. Or was it metempsychosis? Did he know her in another life? He thought of Keats's "La Belle Dame sans Merci." The image of the demon lover had great appeal. Wasn't humankind's oldest universal belief that of sexual intercourse between mortals and supernatural beings? The belief was to be found in most religions and myths.

In early October Roger took a $90 a week room at the Royal Hotel on Granville Street. Lillian wasn't aggrieved by the separation as Roger supposed she'd be. In fact, she accepted it stoically. Her marriage had begun to lose its luster some time ago. As for Jenny, she blamed the breakup on her mother. She was sad to see Roger go.

Now that Roger was on his own it was necessary for him to adapt his lifestyle to his budget. The cost of living in Vancouver was high. Panhandlers, the homeless, hoods, hobos, hookers, homosexuals haunted the downtown streets.

While eating breakfast one morning, Roger read in a newspaper about the latest scientific shortcut to sex. The pheromone face tissue. In London, England, a biotechnology firm had launched a brand of moist tissues soaked in the scent of 50 human pheromones – the sweat molecules responsible for sex appeal. The company said its facial tissues made people appear more attractive to the opposite sex within the radius of one metre for as long as 12 hours. Roger carefully ripped out the news item and stuck it in his pocket.

In the ornate yet gloomy gallery of a castle, Roger was sitting at a table with two men and a woman. They were wearing Venetian carnival masks. Roger felt uncomfortable because he didn't have a mask. One of the men was unashamedly groping the woman and smiling at Roger from time to time. The woman, a big blonde with a beehive hairdo, appeared to enjoy the man's caresses. One of her breasts was exposed, and she kept cooing and tittering all the while. Roger tried not to stare at them. The other man sat there in silence, chain-smoking and constantly glancing up at the vaulted ceiling. Scattered throughout the gallery were other men and women, all in evening dress and half-masked. Roger noticed a woman at a nearby table. She was looking his way. She had on a decollete evening gown, and her breasts bulged out. Suddenly she removed her half mask. Her face was beautiful. Roger smiled at her. Although she was sitting with a man who might have been her husband or an escort, she continued to look beckoningly at Roger. Finally Roger got up and went over to make her acquaintance. As he was introducing himself, he leaned forward and took the liberty of placing his hand lightly on her bare back. Instantly he withdrew his hand in horror. Jutting out of the woman's back like some excrescence, and cold to his touch, was a plucked and headless chicken. The woman grinned, showing big discolored teeth. Roger woke up breathless, frightened, unable to rid his mind of the grotesque image, unable to go back to sleep.

Later that day, while browsing with an actress-friend in a used bookstore, Roger had a jolt of surprise when he came across a dusty, framed picture of a woman whose face bore a striking resemblance to his dream-visitant. He thought it a weird coincidence. The picture – about ten inches by eight – was lying atop a stack of old record albums. He held the picture in his hands and gazed at it lovingly. It was a print of an unsigned painting. The woman was bare-breasted. She had long dark hair, her lips were red, and she was even wearing a red beret. The woman looked like a dancer, interpreting the ecstasy of sex, birth, and death simultaneously. Her provocative pose seemed to force Roger's participation, transforming him from voyeur into sexual partner. Along the border of the picture were tadpole-shaped spermatozoa; and cowering in the lower left corner was a lone human embryo. There was no price tag on the picture. Roger knew he must have it. The proprietor told him the print was of an Edvard Munch lithograph. Roger paid $20 for it. "Does she remind you of someone?" his actress-friend teased him.

Roger hung the picture on the wall above his bed. He spent a great deal of time looking at it, even talking to it, as if it were some idol.

Halloween began inauspiciously for Roger. He woke from a restless sleep in a sullen mood. The morning was foggy. From his fourth-floor window he saw two seagulls standing motionless on an adjacent rooftop. He usually tossed out breadcrusts to the sparrows, starlings, pigeons, crows and seagulls, and watched how they dominated one another. This morning he had no scraps for them.

After finishing his ablutions, he dressed and went out for breakfast. Later that morning, to relieve his glumness, he took a stroll in Stanley Park. In the fog, people appeared like phantoms.

Toward evening there was a fine misty rain. Roger sat in his hotel room, smoking hash and listening to the radio. Since leaving Lillian, he'd had no contact with her. Jenny had phoned him only once. He had expected Lillian to harass him with accusations, or at least beseech him to come back. Her silence dismayed him. He was bored and restless. It was Sunday. He hated Sundays. It was Halloween too. He popped a couple of Valium, slipped on his trench coat, and went out.

He walked over to the Yale Hotel. A band named Dangerous Farm Animals was playing heavy metal rock. A few customers were in Halloween costumes. He drank a rye and Coke and a draft beer, and then he left. His ears were ringing. Outside, he didn't know what to do or where to go next. He felt like a somnambulist.

On Davie Street he thought he saw Jenny. She was wearing a black witch hat and walking toward a parked car. He ducked into a doorway. Yes, he was certain it was Jenny. She removed her hat and climbed into the car. He saw her leaning over to kiss a young man hunched behind the wheel. The car drove off. He noticed it had a vanity plate, with the letters *DREAM*. Wondering if he should phone Lillian, he realized he was standing in front of an erotic lingerie boutique.

"You look lost," a woman's soft voice said suddenly.

"Huh?" Roger turned around and saw a woman of medium height, with a small gift-wrapped package in her hand. The woman was wearing an imitation leopard-skin coat and matching pillbox hat. Her hat and upturned collar partly obscured her face.

"I saw you through the window," the woman said. "I was trying to decide whether you were waiting for someone, or you were too shy to come in."

"Neither," Roger said, taken aback by her playful presumptuousness.

"Then you *are* lost." The warmth of the boutique clung to her like perfume. Although her appearance and manner suggested a certain sophistication, Roger thought for a moment she might be a prostitute.

"Wrong again," he replied. "I just saw my . . . someone I recognized . . . get into a car . . . " He realized how awkward his explanation sounded.

"It happens a lot." The woman smiled. "What if we get into my car and go somewhere for a drink. Or would you rather stand here looking at women's undies?" Her question seemed a challenge.

He struck a pose, and bluffed: "How do you know I'm not some maniac who goes around murdering beautiful women?"

She looked him up and down. "Well, in that case, I won't need a sleeping pill tonight, will I?"

He grinned. "Okay, I'm in your hands," he said, excited yet wondering if she was serious or playing a game with him. He had a good buzz on.

"You look like the trusting type," she said jokingly.

They got into her car, a late-model, black BMW coupe. The interior of the car was so luxurious that Roger refrained from lighting a cigarette. Everything was happening too fast. It all seemed unreal to him. He rolled down the window a few inches to get some air.

"Are you okay?" she asked.

Roger nodded. He noticed she wasn't wearing a wedding ring. He asked her name.

"Lilith."

"Lilith? That's an unusual name."

She shrugged, then smiled. "I'm an unusual woman."

"My name's Roy," he lied.

They drove in silence over the Lion's Gate Bridge, then headed toward North Vancouver. Presently the woman pulled into the underground parking garage of a high-rise apartment building. In the elevator she told him that two friends were visiting her. "They're probably in bed. I went out so they could have a little privacy."

Roger felt higher than the penthouse to which they quickly ascended. The woman's manner became very businesslike.

They entered a spacious, high-ceilinged, richly furnished suite of rooms with wall-to-wall carpeting. Sliding glass doors, with ivory-colored drapes drawn aside, commanded a panoramic view of Burrard Inlet and the glittering lights of the mainland. There was a crystal chandelier dripping with countless pendants. A big fireplace with marble facings. Stained glass. A sunken living room. Roger glanced around, trying to take it all in, awed by the sumptuous furnishings.

"Quite a place," he said, trying to sound casual.

"It's a bit lavish, but I call it home," she said.

He wondered who this strange woman was. He guessed she was the same age as Lillian, maybe a year or two older.

The woman gestured toward a small, mirrored bar across the room. "There's Scotch, gin, vodka, rum, ice. Help yourself. I'll be right back," she added, and disappeared down a dimly lit hallway.

Left alone, he walked over to the bar. He saw a Siamese cat sitting on a Chippendale love seat, watching him. The cat jumped off the seat and slinked into a corner. He poured himself a Scotch on the rocks.

The woman returned shortly, holding a black silk robe on a hanger. She was still in her hat and coat. "Here, put this on," she said, handing him the robe.

"What for?" He hesitated.

"House rule."

"What about your friends?"

She half-smiled. "They're occupied. Put it on. I'll change into something, too," she said as she turned away.

He could not believe what was happening to him. He felt awkward undressing. The woman's behavior was making him wary. He wondered about her two friends. Perhaps she didn't want him to think she was alone. The robe fitted him perfectly. He sipped his drink and gazed out through the glass doors. Orchestral music suddenly began playing. It was Mussorgsky's *Night on Bald Mountain*.

"I could dance with the Devil when I hear that," the woman said as she entered the room.

"Huh?" Startled, he turned and was even more startled by her appearance. Divested of hat and coat, she bore an uncanny resemblance to the woman in his Munch picture. She was wearing a diaphanous bra-gown. Around her neck was a gold chain with a gold Celtic cross hanging upside down. He gazed at her in amazement.

"Happy Halloween!" she said.

"You look beautiful!" he blurted out.

She approached him, took his drink and had a sip of it. On her left wrist was a bracelet of amber and jet. "I've seen you before," she said.

"Where? When?"

She smiled knowingly, and put the glass on a small walnut table. "Come with me," she said, beckoning him with her finger.

As if in a daze, he followed her out of the room. In the hallway he heard a man's voice in one of the rooms. His uncertainty became trepidation.

"Maybe we'll join them later," she said.

The woman's bedroom was huge. In the middle of the room was a big round bed on a dais. The ceiling and two of the walls were mirrors, reflecting both of them myriadfold. A large gilt-framed picture dominated another wall. It showed a goblinish creature squatting on the curvaceous pelvis of an unconscious woman, and a horse's head, with leering eyes, protruding through a drapery.

He gave a little grimace of disgust. "What's that?"

"My nightmare," she said. "A Fuseli print. It belonged to my late husband. He was a psychiatrist." She sat down on the edge of the bed, and undid his robe. "For a man with a big pair of balls, you're not very aggressive."

He stood there, stroking her hair.

"I want you to fuck me," she said.

He was surprised to see that her cunt was shaved. The unexpectedness of it distracted him. He wasn't himself. Was it the Valium? the hash? the booze? his nerves? He wondered. The woman squatted on top of him, grinding her hips; but he was unable to get an erection. He felt tense, embarrassed. He began perspiring. At one point the woman said: "Take your head out of your cock. You're thinking too much." Yet no matter how hard he tried to concentrate, and no matter how skillfully she tried to stimulate him, the reality of his fantasy faded. His penis remained limp. He saw the dark look of perplexity and disappointment on her face. He sensed her cold impatience.

Finally she said in a testy voice: "Get me a drink. Anything. With ice."

He had to urinate but was too humiliated to ask her where the bathroom was.

Out in the hallway he heard half-articulated sounds, moans. He held his breath at the door of the room, listening. The door was slightly ajar. He sneaked a look inside.

Shock. Disbelief.

He saw reflected in a large mirror a big fleshy woman in a black domino mask. She was on her hands and knees, her head bobbing wildly, grunting in unison with some man in a death's-head mask who was mounting her forcefully and rhythmically from behind.

I'm hallucinating! he thought.

The woman looked like his estranged wife.

BY THE AUTHOR

FICTION

A Christmas for Carol
Blind Spot

POETRY

Halo of Flies
Chthonic Light
I Once Had a Pet Praying Mantis
Selected Poems
Ink from an Octopus
The Climate of the Heart
Breaking and Entering
Moon Without Light
If You Love
One Bullet Left

DRAMA

Enough Rope

EDITOR

Acknowledgment to Life: The Collected Poems of
Bertram Warr